"Captured"

M/M Viking Historical Gay Romance

Jerry Cole

Disclaimer

This book is intended for adults (18+) only. The contents may be offensive to some readers. It contains graphic language, explicit sexual content, and adult situations. Please do not read this book if you are offended by such content or if you are under the age of 18. All sexually active characters are 18+.

This is a work of fiction. Names, characters, businesses, places, events and incidents are either the products of the author's imagination or used in a fictitious manner & are not to be construed as real. Any resemblance to actual persons, living or dead, or actual events is purely coincidental.

Cover images are licensed stock photos, images shown for illustrative purposes only. Any person(s) that may be depicted on the cover are models.

Edition v1.00 (2016.07.10)
http://www.jerrycoleauthor.com

Chapter One

Spring was alive in Arnnstead, birdsong bright and lyrical illuminating the chilly breeze. Sunlight sparkled on the un-melted snow still crusted in shadowed patches on the ground, speared through with tender grass and early flowers. The sky was a piercing blue so bright it almost hurt to look at, stacked with thick, rolling white clouds which might bring light rain or late snows or only drifting shade. In the village, life hummed with newborn vibrancy after the dreary silence of a long winter, everyone rushing to tasks long neglected in those icy days.

"Einarr!"

Aiden gasped his lover's name, gripping the low, wide bench they slept on tightly just to hold himself in place against the fierce thrusts of the powerful man behind him. Part of him wanted to ask Einarr to be a little gentler, but they'd been holding back for months, and to be honest, he was just as desperate as the other man.

A thick fur protected his knees from the wooden bench, and Aiden buried his face in it to stifle his gasps as Einarr drove into him, filling him to his limit, pounding relentlessly, sending shocks of pleasure up his spine with every strike. His back bowed as a particularly rough one left stars dancing in his eyes.

Einarr was normally far gentler, but they were both a little wild in their passions today. They'd begun their relationship in earnest only a season ago, and had found it stifled quickly by the necessities of winter. Einarr shared a one-room longhouse with his sister-in-law, her mother, and the daughter of his first marriage. And during winter, they also shared it with a host of goats— not terribly romantic settings for a new love. Today, the first proper day of spring, the goats had been moved back outside, the women were all elsewhere, and they at last had the freedom to indulge in one another without fear of notice. And they had been indulging heavily.

Einarr pulled out suddenly to grab Aiden's waist and turn him to lie on his back. Aiden stared up at the handsome, kind-eyed blond man above him, surprised, and then abruptly lost his ability to focus as Einarr surged back in.

"I want to see your face," Einarr rumbled, bending to kiss him soundly, his beard scratching Aiden's skin. An intricately carved wooden bead was woven into that beard, and a similar one hung from a braid in Aiden's hair. They were the symbols of their devotion to each other, in lieu of the more traditional symbols they were denied by the nature of their relationship.

Aiden clung to Einarr's shoulders, his face flushed and his brow furrowed with unfocused ecstasy as Einarr continued to drive into him, shaking his body with every strike. Realizing Einarr was staring at him, Aiden hid his face with an arm, embarrassed, but Einarr dragged it away quickly, pinning Aiden's wrist near his head.

"Don't hide." Einarr's voice was low and ragged with desire. "I want to see it. I want to see all of you."

4

He punctuated his statements with deep, lingering thrusts that made Aiden cry out his name, quaking in the older man's arms. Einarr stifled them with deep kisses, each one filled with emotion that made it clear to Aiden just how much his lover, once captor, adored him.

They'd met in late summer, when Aiden had lived in an English village as a sheepherder, miserable and resigned to misery. But that village was burned by Einarr and the other Viking men of Arnnstead. Aiden would have died with it, but Einarr saved him by claiming Aiden as a thrall, a slave. Aiden had hated Einarr in those early days. But time had quickly brought them closer, and danger closer still, until through brave deeds, Aiden had earned enough silver to buy his own freedom. Now a freedman and Einarr's equal, their devotion to each other had only grown.

Einarr's hand wrapped around Aiden's shaft, making Aiden gasp, his hips jerking up into the contact as pleasure crashed over him like a wave and built toward a tsunami that would sweep him away. Einarr caught Aiden's hand, lacing their fingers together as they both fell like stars toward earth. Aiden felt Einarr throb inside him as the other man pulled him close, holding on to him tightly, delving as deeply into him as he was capable. Aiden squeezed Einarr's hand as he felt the spreading warmth of the other man's completion inside him. Einarr continued to stroke Aiden, and a few moments later, Einarr still inside him, Aiden shuddered and finished as well, clinging to Einarr breathlessly. Einarr pressed a delicate kiss to Aiden's temple, then slowly pulled out and began to clean them both up while Aiden laid where he'd been left, trying to catch his breath. They had made very thorough use of this morning together, and Aiden knew he'd feel it in his back later. Not that he minded. He glanced over at Einarr, pulling his pants on, and smiled at the sight of him, built broad and muscular, with kind blue eyes and hair the color of warm honey. Einarr glanced over when he noticed Aiden staring and smiled back, the expression full of undisguised affection. He finished pulling up his pants, then bent to kiss Aiden again.

"Are you going to be able to walk?" he asked, barely moving back far enough to leave an inch between them. "We have a lot to do today. But if I've broken you, I don't mind explaining to the men that you needed a day to recover."

Aiden blushed in embarrassment, pushing Einarr away with a scoff. The other man only laughed through his lover's struggle to avoid him, kissing him again.

"Just give me a minute," Aiden grumbled. "You were really rough that last time."

"I'm sorry," Einarr's voice was warm with love as he brushed Aiden's hair back from his face. "I've been wanting it so long, I suppose I lost control of myself."

"I didn't mind that much," Aiden confessed, glancing away, red hair falling in front of his eyes. Einarr grinned and kissed him again, and Aiden, unable to resist, caught the other man by the back of the head to return it and deepen it. Einarr leaned in closer, hand tangling in Aiden's hair. Aiden gave a breathy little moan into the kiss as Einarr's fingers grazed his scalp, and Einarr pulled abruptly away with a groan.

"It isn't fair of you to make sounds like that," he complained. "We do have to go out and get *some* work done today."

Aiden grinned, his finger trailing down Einarr's chest.

"The work can wait a little bit longer."

They did eventually make it outside, though Aiden wasn't walking quite normally, and Einarr had a dreamy, distracted expression that made it obvious what they had been up to. Fortunately, their relationship was something of an open secret. It wasn't something to be spoken of in polite conversation, but the Norse, and in particular the people of Arnnstead, took little issue with men having those kinds of relationships with each other. Especially in the case of a man like Einarr, who'd been married and had children already, and thus had done his duty to his family. What they did take issue with was one man submitting to another in the way of women. Aiden, who had been Einarr's thrall and who even now, as a freedman, was still bound to Einarr by tradition, was expected to submit to Einarr, so it was less shameful than if two free men had engaged in such a relationship. But Aiden still endured some mockery and mistrust as the assumed receptive partner. Einarr did his best to shield Aiden from it, but

Aiden didn't mind so much. It was tiring, true, but very little to pay, in his eyes, for a relationship that brought him so much happiness. In the devoutly Christian village he'd been raised in, things would have been much more unpleasant.

Together, they ambled up toward the fields the villagers all worked. They grew barley and oats and vegetables, and it was just the beginning of the planting season now. As they climbed the hill, a tall, long-limbed man with wild, dark hair paused to wave at them.

"Look at this, Branulf!" the man shouted to a stockier, more sullen-faced man beside him. "They made it out of bed before noon, after all! I owe you a drink."

"I would have stayed all day, Faralder, but I kept thinking of your hideous face and spoiling things," Einarr teased back as they approached. Faralder took a playful swing at the blond man, which became a hug that was half a grapple.

"Good morning, Branulf." Aiden waved at the shorter man. "Sorry for being late. Is everything going well so far?"

Aiden had been going out of his way lately to try and be sociable with Branulf. The man— one of Einarr's oldest friends— hadn't approved of Aiden at all when Einarr had brought him here. Though Branulf had come to accept the relationship, they were still trying to warm up to each other slowly.

"Morning," Branulf replied stiffly, watching Einarr and Faralder, who were now all but wrestling. "The ground has thawed already."

"That's a good sign." Aiden smiled, relieved, and stepped out of the way as Einarr and Faralder hit the ground, rolling over one another. "The planting should go quickly, then."

"The sooner the fields are planted for the year," Branulf agreed, "The sooner we'll be free to go raiding."

Aiden hummed in agreement, but to be honest, the thought worried him. The Northmen would go Viking all through summer, returning in fall to help with the harvest and be with their families through winter. Since he'd been captured during the last raid of fall, this would be the first raiding season since he'd come to live here. He knew he'd be expected to join them during the raiding, and he didn't want to be separated from Einarr that long anyway; the thought of raiding, however, especially along the English coast as they had done last year and probably would again, made nervous guilt squirm in Aiden's stomach. He wasn't confident he could burn villages he could easily have been born in. What if they met someone he knew, someone he'd grown up with? To the Northmen, raiding was honorable. A fair fight in which the winner took all. But Aiden had difficulty seeing it that way. He'd never had to fight when he wasn't defending his own life before.

As Aiden was lost in thought, Branulf turned his hoe around to prod the stick end in between Einarr and Faralder, scolding them for wasting time when there was so much to be done. The two sprang apart laughing, promising to finish their scuffle later, and they all returned to work, preparing the fields for planting.

So it would be for most of spring. Waking early, they washed every morning before breakfast. Einarr had a fondness for combing Aiden's hair for him, though his sister in law, Jódís, thought it was indecent and wouldn't let Agna, his seven year old daughter, watch. Apparently, it was considered rather an intimate thing to do for someone. Aiden had insisted on being allowed to comb Einarr's hair for him when he'd learned this, but he'd yanked on so many knots that they'd both decided it might be better to leave it up to Einarr in the future.

After breakfast, Jódís and Agna would leave to tend the animals and Einarr's aged mother-in-law would toddle off to the longhouse to weave with the other old women. Depending on what needed doing, once the animals were fed, Jódís and Agna might join her there, or out in the fields to help with the planting.

Einarr and Aiden stole all the quiet moments together they could. It became a kind of game, figuring out when they could escape together and to what discrete places. Kisses stolen when no one was looking were all the sweeter for it.

Spring continued to warm the earth, bringing bright flowers and a wealth of game and life to the hills. In the easy, peaceful flow of days and the passion of a still young and tender romance, it was easy for Aiden to forget what was coming closer with the slow approach of summer.

"Have you heard the news of Jarl Bjorn?"

In the evenings, such as tonight, the men gathered in the longhouse, the women's looms put away, to eat and drink and discuss the future. A matter which, for them, seemed primarily concerned with when and where they would eventually go raiding. As such, Aiden would generally tune it out, but the mention of Jarl Bjorn caught his attention.

It was Faralder who brought it up, sitting near Einarr and Aiden, Branulf on the other side of them, their respective families scattered about in-between. Faralder's family was enormous. He had two wives, a concept that had shocked Aiden speechless when he'd first arrived, and more children than Aiden could readily count— not to mention the various aunts and uncles and grandparents who shared his house as well. Einarr was unusual for having so few people in his house, but Faralder was the opposite extreme.

"Has he gone conquering again?" Einarr asked in mild concern. "Surely he wouldn't call his men to war before the planting is done."

"It's precisely that he hasn't that is the news," Faralder replied. "Apparently, he has no intention of claiming any more villages. Arnnjorn must have talked some sense into him after what happened last winter. He says he'll gather his armies in summer to go raiding in Vinland, but he's claimed all he will of the homeland."

"I thought he intended to be king of all Midgard," Branulf said with a scoff. "I bet that son of his hasn't taken the news well."

Aiden thought back to last winter, to cold, grim-faced Jarl Bjorn and his pompous, overly ambitious son, Hallvaror. The Jarl had been set on uniting all the people of the North under his banner and had set his sights on Arnnstead. When Arnnjorn— their chief and Einarr's uncle— refused to bend the knee, he'd promised war. And it was a war Arnnstead was bound to lose, but chose to fight anyway, rather than give up their independence without a struggle. They'd been saved a conflict with Bjorn when a short-lived surprise attack by the English had threatened not just Arnnstead, but all of the coastal villages, especially those left undefended because their men were all away in the Jarl's army. In return for their help in stopping the English attack there, the Jarl had promised to leave Arnnstead in peace. And apparently the ferocity of their fighting had impressed the Jarl so much that he'd decided perhaps uniting would weaken rather than strengthen the north.

"Well, that's one less threat to worry about," Einarr said, sounding relieved. "With the English growing bolder in attacking the settlements in Northumbria, we could use fewer enemies."

"We could," Branulf agreed solemnly, "But I don't think we'll get them. Without the threat of Bjorn's army hanging over our heads, the smaller clans will turn to raiding each other again as we always have."

12

"Well, where else can we look for a decent fight?" Faralder answered him with a laugh. "The English certainly aren't up to it. No offense, Aiden."

"None taken."

Aiden shrugged, not feeling attached enough to his homeland to defend it from such a petty jab.

Conversation turned then, inevitably, to raiding and what villages they might challenge now that so many were under Bjorn's banner and thus more or less untouchable. Faralder was all for attacking those villages anyway, but luckily, he was in the minority in that matter.

Aiden tuned out again, his thoughts wandering, until Einarr's hand on his shoulder alerted him to most of the men filtering out back to their homes for the night. Aiden shook his head to clear his thoughts and joined his lover in heading home, bidding farewell to Faralder and Branulf on the way. At home, the wide, fur-strewn benches that lined the sides of the longhouse looked warm and inviting. Agna and Jódís were already asleep among the furs, so Aiden felt less embarrassed than usual to climb in beside Einarr. He always felt safest and slept the best when his back was pressed to Einarr's chest and he was held in the other man's arms. But occasionally, when Jódís was glaring at them disapprovingly from across the fire, he couldn't bring himself to do it, though Einarr didn't care. Jódís wasn't a bad person and was quite cordial to Aiden at most times, but neither did she hide the fact that she thought the relationship was inappropriate, especially when they dared to show their affection in front of Agna. It got tiring, but Aiden held out hope that, with time, Jódís would get used to the relationship and cease making such a fuss about it.

In the meantime, he was content to end most days exactly like this— Einarr holding him close, breath warm on the back of his neck, a quiet assurance that Aiden was exactly where he was meant to be.

Chapter Two

The days of spring rushed past in exactly this way, until the day a man Aiden had never seen rode into town. It was still early on a Saturday, and Aiden and Einarr were just returning from bathing in the hot spring up the hill when the stranger arrived.

"Who is that?" Aiden asked curiously as the man swung off his horse and marched toward the longhouse. "I don't recognize him."

Einarr frowned as Aiden pointed the man out, confusion and concern on his face.

"I believe that is Olvaldr," Einarr replied, "Arnnjorn's sister's husband. He lives with her in a village further inland. I wonder what he is doing here without her."

"Why do I get the feeling it's not going to be good news?" Aiden asked, uneasy.

Sure enough, later that evening, Arnnjorn's expression grim, he called all the men of the village into the longhouse. Being the central building of the town, its bare wooden beams and pillars crawled with carvings of heroes and gods, dancing in the warm light of torches and the central fireplace. Arnnjorn Eagle-Bear, massive and red-bearded, presided over all from a fur draped throne at the far end of the hall, frowning over his hands in undisguised displeasure, like nothing so much as a statue of some severe heathen god in an ancient temple.

"My beloved sister Etta of Haurhall is dead," Arnnjorn announced, to the sympathetic murmurs of the men. "Murdered by men of Ingifast who beset her on the road, betraying all law and honor by slaying an unarmed woman who had done them no wrong."

Sympathy turned to outrage in an instant, and even Aiden felt a moment of horrified shock. There were few greater crimes to the Northmen than to commit violence against a woman. Women were not allowed to carry weapons, so to harm a woman was always an act of cowardice. In the sagas, which Einarr had been sharing with Aiden a story at a time, a man was fined two ounces of gold for giving a woman four unwanted kisses. Later in the story, he was justly killed by that same woman. Such things were not tolerated.

"Her husband has come to me today to ask my aid in avenging himself upon Ingifast for her death," Arnnjorn continued. "I come to you to ask if you will join me in laying in the soil every male relative of the monstrous cowards who murdered my sister."

The resounding shout of agreement shook the hall and left no doubt. Aiden's heart raced with realization of what this would mean. A raid, and one for vengeance, in fact. Would he be expected to join? He assumed so. He supposed it was better than a raid on the English, but anxiety still gripped him, unsure if he could bring himself to kill someone that wasn't actively trying to kill him. He tried to reassure himself that, if they stormed the village, there would almost certainly be plenty of people actively trying to kill him, but it was a cold comfort.

Arnnjorn called several men to help him plan the attack, including Einarr. Aiden and the other men were left to return to their work, all of them murmuring excitedly about the raid. Most of them went to sharpen their weapons and strengthen their shields. Aiden went to the fields to continue planting instead, fearing his stomach would turn if he had to handle weapons of war just now.

"Aiden!"

He looked up when someone called out to him as he was approaching the field. It was Jódís, frowning with concern. Branulf and Faralder's wives stood behind her, and he could see other women, still tending the fields, watching them curiously.

"What was said in the longhouse?" Jódís demanded. "What news did Olvaldr bring?"

"Arrnjorn's sister has been murdered," Aiden reported. "Arnnjorn is organizing a raid in revenge."

Jódís's eyes widened, and the other women fell to worried chatter immediately.

"A raid against Ingifast?" Jódís asked, pale. "What did Einarr say?"

Aiden frowned in confusion.

"Nothing," he replied. "Arnnjorn called him to discuss strategy with the others, but he didn't say anything to me. Why would he?"

"You don't know?" Jódís seemed genuinely surprised by Aiden's confusion. "Einarr was born in Ingifast."

Aiden was taken aback by this. He'd never thought to ask Einarr where he was born. He'd just

17

assumed it was here in Arnnstead. He was surprised Einarr had never brought it up himself.

As the women got back to work, all of them talking anxiously of the raid to come, Aiden's own troubled thoughts were full of Einarr. How could they expect him to attack the place he'd been born? What if he still had family that lived there? And again and again his thoughts wandered idly back to the fact that he hadn't known where Einarr was born. He realized in thinking about it further that he knew fairly little about Einarr's past, actually. He knew Einarr had been married, but not the name of his wife or what their relationship had been like. He knew Einarr had a brother who was killed in a raid, but little else. He knew Einarr loved skyr, a kind of delicious mild yogurt, and hated waking too early in the morning. What else did he know? It shocked him to realize how little he could list that was not meaningless trivia. They'd been together more than half a year. Shouldn't they know each other better?

He went on worrying about it until late into the evening. He went home with Jódís when the light failed, and she made dinner for everyone. Agna, who'd taken an instant liking to Aiden when he'd arrived, sat next to Aiden and babbled excitedly about a dream she'd had. Aiden nodded along, preoccupied with his thoughts. Would Einarr tell him these things if he just asked? Or was there a reason it hadn't been brought up? Aiden had thought his fears of Einarr tiring of him and discarding him had been eliminated when he'd purchased his freedom, but those worries came roaring back now, and Aiden struggled to put them away.

Einarr returned late, when Aiden was the last person still up, dozing off by the fire as he waited.

"You're back," Aiden mumbled, rubbing his eyes as Einarr entered. "I saved dinner for you."

"Thank you, Aiden," Einarr said tiredly, shambling past him toward the bench. "But I ate in the hall. I just want to sleep."

"What was decided?" Aiden asked, putting Einarr's food aside and coming to join him. "Will we leave tomorrow?"

"In a few days," Einarr replied shortly, rolling over with his back to Aiden, dragging the furs over himself, "Once the planting is far enough along that the women can handle the rest."

Aiden hesitated, not used to Einarr brushing him off like that. Slightly unsure, he laid down beside the other man anyway.

"Did you really used to live in Ingifast?" Aiden asked, pulling up a fur for himself so he wouldn't have to pull any away from Einarr.

"Who told you that?" Einarr's voice was unexpectedly sharp, and Aiden flinched.

"Jódís mentioned it," he explained, uneasy. Einarr said nothing, and Aiden couldn't see his expression.

"Will you be okay?" he asked, pressing for Einarr to talk to him even if the man seemed to be in some kind of mood. "Raiding somewhere you used to live?"

"Of course I will." Einarr didn't hesitate that time. "I'm a man, aren't I?"

There were only a few inches between them, but to Aiden, it suddenly felt like a wide gulf. He wasn't used to Einarr acting this way. The warrior was usually an expert at bottling up his feelings behind a laugh and a smile. He was still hiding something, but rather than playing it off with a joke, he'd chosen this brusque hostility, and Aiden didn't know what that meant. He was struck again with just how little he really knew about the other man. His frustration and worry made a complicated knot in his gut.

"Did something happen?" he pushed, reaching out to touch Einarr's shoulder. "If you would just tell me—"

"Nothing happened," Einarr insisted, twitching away from the touch. "Go to sleep."

Aiden's anxious worry boiled into annoyance.

"Fine then," he hissed. "Keep it to yourself."

He rolled over, putting his back to Einarr and pulling the fur tight around him. If the other man wanted to throw a temper tantrum, he could go right ahead. Aiden tried to ignore the hurt throbbing in his chest. Was it wrong of him to want to know more about the man he was in love with?

Chapter Three

Aiden woke the next morning groggy and on edge. He hadn't slept well, and his anxious fears were still buzzing around like a nest of angry hornets in his stomach. Jódís was already up, stirring up the fire for breakfast while Agna went to get water for them to clean with. Einarr nudged Aiden's shoulder to hurry him out of bed, and Aiden rolled out grumbling, the fur still around his shoulders.

"Do you really think Agna's old enough to fetch water on her own?" Einarr asked, his gaze preoccupied, staring off into space.

"She's nearly eight," Jódís replied, stirring the oats they would have for breakfast. "I'd be surprised if she couldn't handle something that simple."

Einarr hummed, thoughts still far away. He seemed less cranky this morning, Aiden thought, but now he was distracted. Aiden wanted to ask what he was thinking about, but he was afraid to receive the same kind of reaction as last night. The helpless worry only drove his frustrated annoyance higher.

After breakfast, they passed around the water basin and the comb. When they reached Aiden, Einarr gestured for him to come closer.

"Let me comb your hair for you," he offered, smiling like nothing happened. Aiden generally enjoyed Einarr doing his hair. But today, the thought of sitting there annoyed him. He shook his head.

"I can manage it myself."

It came out sharper than he'd meant it to, and he saw a flash of hurt in Einarr's eyes. He tried to ignore it, and the corresponding flare of pain in his own chest. Einarr would survive not doing his hair for one day until Aiden's annoyance faded.

They headed out to the fields next, and Aiden hung on to the hope that maybe, as they worked, Einarr would get the hint and just tell Aiden what was bothering him. But Einarr said nothing, leaving Aiden so frustrated and distracted, he nearly cut his own leg open with the hoe. At last, Faralder took the tool out of his hands.

"That's enough," the tall, scraggly-bearded man declared. "I'm not going to watch you lame yourself over whatever little tiff you and Einarr are in."

"Don't be ridiculous," Aiden griped, snatching for the hoe. "I've got to work."

"Tell me what's going on first, and I'll give it back," Faralder said childishly, holding it out of Aiden's reach.

"Nothing is going on!" Aiden snapped, jumping for it. "Let me work!"

"I haven't seen you this wound up since the day we took you out of England," Faralder countered, easily keeping the hoe out of Aiden's reach. "Now, tell me the truth."

Aiden huffed in irritation and gave up, throwing his hands in the air and stomping away to the edge of the field. He stared down at the town, uneasy irritation turning his stomach. He couldn't seem to choose one or the other, flashing back and forth

22

between anger and fear. He wanted to shake Einarr and make him explain. At the same time, the thought of pushing the other man away terrified him. But on the other hand, if he said nothing, what if this gap between them kept growing? They couldn't just maintain a relationship where neither of them knew anything about each other. If Einarr would just *tell* him... And then he'd be back to the anger again. But now, looking down on the town he'd come to care about so much— specifically because it was the place he could be together with Einarr— all he felt was sadness. He should have realized he couldn't go on being this happy. It was bound to fall apart eventually. It was only just now starting to crumble around the edges, but Aiden could see what would happen and how it would ruin them...

He sank down into the grass, pulling his knees up to his chest. A moment later, Faralder sat down beside him.

"You know I'm your friend, don't you?" Faralder asked. "Maybe you're not familiar with what having friends is like, but generally, you rely on them for help and advice when you're upset. I understand if that's a confusing concept where you're from. Englishmen only make friends with sheep, right?"

Aiden scowled at the other man, who only grinned broadly. Aiden huffed, looking back out at the view.

"Lately, I've just been thinking about the fact that I don't really fit here," Aiden admitted, picking at the grass absentmindedly. "I'm trying, but... Everyone

23

knows about me and Einarr, and so that's complicated. I'm never sure what's expected of me, where I should be, or what I should be doing. I try to just follow Einarr's lead, but he takes it easy on me, and I think others resent me for it. I don't learn very fast and I don't understand things everyone else does. I get in the way. And recently..."

He trailed off, hunching his shoulders guiltily that he was admitting this out loud.

"Recently, I've started to wonder if maybe I'm not as close to Einarr as I thought I was."

Aiden looked back at the field, where Einarr was still working near Branulf. He'd been preoccupied all day, so distracted he hadn't even noticed Aiden leave. Faralder put a comforting hand on Aiden's shoulder.

"Einarr can be difficult sometimes," Faralder shrugged, looking back out over the view. "He's very open about some things, but then you ask the wrong question, and suddenly, what you thought was an open door turns into a stone wall."

"Yesterday, I learned that he was born in the town we're going to raid," Aiden explained, "And he came home from meeting with Arnnjorn about it looking upset. But when I tried to ask, he shut me out. Now I'm afraid to ask again."

"Einarr would never want you to be afraid of him," Faralder frowned, concerned. "I'm certain he would never harm you."

"I'm not afraid of him," Aiden explained, gripping his knees tighter to his chest. "I'm afraid of losing him. What would happen to me if Einarr got tired of me? Where would I go?"

Faralder's hand on Aiden's shoulder tightened, and his concerned frown grew deeper, staring off at the horizon.

"I don't know anything about Einarr's life in Ingifast," Faralder said, "Only that he was already a young man when he came here, and that it hurts him to remember that place. But I think if there's anyone he would tell, it would be you. I'm certain that, if you talk to him, tell him the things you are afraid of, he will open up to you. There is no one closer to him than you."

Aiden looked away, worried by that. If there was no one closer than him, and he barely knew Einarr at all, how alone must Einarr be?

He decided that he would ask Einarr tonight, but Arnnjorn called the warrior in for another long strategic talk. Aiden waited as long as he could, but by the time Einarr returned, Aiden had long since fallen asleep. When he woke the next morning, he found Einarr sleeping on a different bench. The gulf between them felt wider than ever.

"We'll be leaving today," Einarr announced at breakfast, catching Aiden by surprise.

"So soon?" Jódís asked. "I thought you would wait longer."

"The fields are plowed," Einarr replied through his porridge. "The hardest part is done. I trust you to take care of everything else, Jódís."

The uneasy knot in Aiden's chest doubled in size, and he struggled to swallow his food past the lump in his throat.

After they had finished and begun washing, Einarr caught Aiden's hand to pull him closer.

"Let me comb your hair today?"

Aiden, feeling guilty for refusing yesterday, nodded reluctantly and sat on the floor between the other man's knees. Einarr's hands were gentle and attentive as he washed and brushed out Aiden's red hair.

"It's grown longer," Einarr observed, running his fingers through the fire-colored curls. "It only came to your nape when I met you."

It was down around his collar now, almost long enough to braid. Einarr, presumably thinking the same thing, began twisting small braids into the side of Aiden's hair.

Jódís and Agna and her grandmother had already left since Aiden was always last to wash. So he and Einarr had privacy as the other man's fingers grazed his scalp, gentle and soothing.

"Thank you for letting me do this," Einarr said. "Since there will be fighting today, I wanted to be certain I could do this one last time."

"Don't be ridiculous," Aiden scoffed to hide his worry. "You'll be fine. I'll be there to guard your back."

Einarr's hands paused in Aiden's hair like this had surprised him.

"I am coming with you, aren't I?" Aiden turned to look at the other man seriously. Einarr looked unsure, not meeting his gaze.

"Perhaps it would be better if you did not," he said. "No one will expect you to, knowing what you are."

"What I am?" Aiden moved away from Einarr entirely. "Which is?"

"Aiden..."

"Wasn't I ready to fight when Jarl Branulf was coming for us?" Aiden bristled with anger. "Didn't I fight when the village was attacked? Am I not a warrior the same as you?"

Einarr didn't answer, looking away. Aiden felt a pang of shame. He knew some of the other men in the village considered Aiden less for being an argr— a man who took a woman's role in sex. There were others that just looked down on him for being English. But he'd never counted Einarr among them.

He hadn't wanted this morning to go like this. He still wanted to talk to Einarr, close this widening gap between them.

"Einarr," he said quietly, still kneeling at Einarr's feet, his hand on the other man's thigh, "Would you tell me what happened in Ingifast? Why did you move here to live in your uncle's village? I can tell it upsets you. I want to know everything about you, Einarr. The good things and the bad..."

Einarr's jaw tightened, and he was silent for a long moment, considering it. Aiden was perplexed by the fear he saw in Einarr's eyes. Was what had

27

happened truly so bad that the thought of telling someone frightened him?

At last, Einarr sighed and reached out to run his fingers through Aiden's hair again.

"I can't tell you now." His fingers brushed the shell of Aiden's ear as he brushed back those red curls. "I wouldn't want it to affect your judgement when we go there. After all, I need you to be guarding my back."

He smiled hopefully, trying to make peace, and Aiden reluctantly accepted it, leaning into Einarr's touch.

"Fine," Aiden agreed, "But when we get back, you will tell. That, and other things too. I want to know the man I'm in love with."

"Then it's a deal," Einarr agreed, and pulled Aiden up into his lap to kiss him. "I'll answer all the questions you can think of as soon as we get home. Now, go and sharpen your axe. We'll be leaving soon."

Aiden lingered a moment longer to kiss Einarr again, thinking about the way his stomach always fluttered with excitement whenever Einarr's lips brushed his. No matter how many times he kissed the other man, it always felt like the first kiss. The solution they had reached didn't quite satisfy him, but at least they were no longer fighting. That was enough for Aiden, at least for now. All his fears of being abandoned and having no place remained, but perhaps, for the sake of Einarr, he could ignore them for a little while longer.

They went together to prepare their weapons and ensure they were prepared for the overland raid. Aiden had received an axe of his own now that he was no longer a thrall and was allowed to carry one. But for this situation, Einarr gave Aiden his axe anyway, which was more finely made, and Einarr used the sword passed down to him by Arnnjorn. It was one of only two swords in the village, the other belonging to Arnnjorn himself. Everyone else did just fine with axes and clubs. Aiden had been training a little, learning to use his axe better than just swinging wildly with it, though that hadn't been ineffective when they'd defended the village from the English last winter. But still, he felt woefully underprepared, watching the other men who'd been training all their lives and who had raided so many times before this. And they wouldn't be fighting poorly trained, badly organized English, but other Northmen, trained the same as they were. It all made Aiden very anxious and unsure of himself, as if he hadn't already been unsure to begin with.

As the sun climbed higher, warming the morning that was still chill for late spring, the men gathered before the longhouse and prepared to leave. Arnnjorn's brother-in-law raised horses— small, sturdy things that Aiden would have called a pony in comparison to English horses, and he'd brought a pack of them, though not enough for everyone to ride. Arnnjorn and the other chief warriors he'd chosen to lead them each took a horse, and the others were used to carry supplies, because Ingifast was more than a day's ride away. They'd camp on the way there, well clear of the settlement so they wouldn't be spotted too soon, then attack the next day.

Einarr and Aiden didn't speak much as they prepared. Einarr was too preoccupied with organizing the march. Arnnjorn had put more responsibility than usual on his nephew, perhaps because he sensed the day was coming when he would hand over leadership of Arnnstead to Einarr. Everyone knew Einarr was Arnnjorn's only heir, his other sons having died before him, but Arnnjorn was still strong and healthy, one of the mightiest warriors in the village, and so talk of Einarr's eventual leadership did not often come up.

When everything was ready, the raiding party left with surprisingly little ceremony. There would be a celebration if they came back victorious, but their departure was quiet, almost solemn. Perhaps it was only so reserved because they were on a mission of revenge. Perhaps the next time they went out, things would be more jovial. Aiden wasn't certain if that would be better or worse.

They rode out over the hills, the chief and his strongest warriors leading on their horses. The rest of the men, perhaps sixty including Aiden, ran behind them, all their thoughts on the battle ahead of them. Aiden jogged to try and keep up with Einarr's horse, never straying far. He was feeling the same fear he'd experienced the last time he'd fought beside the other man, unable to shake the feeling that, if he let Einarr out of his sight, something terrible would happen and he'd never see his lover again. They hadn't even begun to fight yet, but already, anxiety clutched Aiden's chest like a vice. He tried to shake it off, knowing he needed to focus on the raid. But he couldn't help resenting whatever it was about the Northmen that compelled them to be constantly throwing themselves into violence.

They rode through the rest of the day and well into the evening, until it became too dark to keep secure footing on the rocky, icy slopes of the hills. At last, Arnnjorn stopped them on a small hill near a cliff where they'd have shelter as well as a good view.

"Make camp here for the night," he ordered. "No fires. Ingifast is only an hour's ride that way. In the first light of dawn, we'll burn them before they've even crawled from their beds."

A short cheer went up from the men before they began settling in for the night. Aiden found Einarr as the warriors sat with their backs to the cliff, which was a convenient place to sleep at the ready, their weapons at hand. Aiden sat down beside the other man with a tired sigh. Walking all day and carrying his weapons had been more tiring than he'd expected.

"How is everything looking so far?" Aiden asked, leaning so that their shoulders met. "Still too early to tell?"

"There's been no problems so far," Einarr answered, frowning down at his sword across his knees. "But that's no guarantee that things will be fine tomorrow. I've planned for all I can, and now all I can really do is pray the gods are with us."

"Sounds stressful," Aiden frowned, concerned for the other man. "Are you handling it alright?"

Einarr sighed and unselfconsciously dropped his head onto Aiden's shoulder.

"I don't know how Arnnjorn does it," he replied, sounding exhausted, "And I have no idea how I'm meant to do it one day as well."

"You have plenty of time to figure it out," Aiden promised reassuringly, smiling down at the man leaning on him, even though it was embarrassing to have Einarr doing this in front of the other men. "Arnnjorn will be around for a long time yet. Just try to learn what you can. This is a good opportunity."

Aiden, caught up in his own worries, hadn't noticed that Einarr had nagging concerns of his own, which Aiden could only guess at. One more thing about Einarr he didn't really know. He supposed he'd ask after the raid, like everything else. He tried not to let his irritation at having to wait spoil this moment. Not to mention the obvious worry that they might not make it back from this at all. He reached down to catch Einarr's hand, if only to comfort himself. The gesture seemed to surprise Einarr, but he smiled as he laced their fingers, hidden between them from the judgmental gaze of the other men. They would get through this, Aiden promised himself. After everything else they'd been through, it wouldn't be this that broke them, he was certain.

Chapter Four

In the morning, there was a palpable jangle of nerves through the camp. Most of the men were excited, or put up fronts to appear so, eager to prove their strength and bravery in battle. Eager to die, if it proved to be their time, and join the warriors of legend in the halls of the victorious dead. It was one of the Norse ideals Aiden was having the most difficulty accepting. To Arnnjorn's warriors, the time of their death was already set. They would die the moment the gods had ordained they would do so, and until that time they were, for all intents and purposes, invincible. Why not then throw themselves into battle with zero regard for their own safety? Aiden no longer believed in the Christian god he'd been raised with, but neither had he accepted Einarr's gods, and he couldn't be so content with allowing them to choose the moment he died. He'd rather that he and those he cared about live as long as they could under their own power.

Still, Aiden could tell that the faith was not so rock solid in all of Arnnjorn's warriors. Or at least, some of them worried their gods might have chosen today to be their end and weren't quite ready to meet the Valkyrie yet. Some were too loud, trying too hard, or else snapping and lashing out in annoyance at any small irritation to their already raw nerves. Some were too quiet, their thoughts preoccupied. Aiden was surprised to see Arnnjorn was one of these. The massive, red-bearded man stared pensively into the distance, muttering snatches of poetry under his breath as though he saw something grim in the gray, misted morning.

"Cried then the berserks, carnage they had thoughts of," Aiden leaned closer to hear the old man reciting, "Wailed then the wolf-coated and weapons brandished..."

Aiden shivered and turned away. There was a skald, a poet and storyteller, who had wintered in Arnnstead and spent most nights in the longhouse reciting the stories of the Northmen. Aiden had enjoyed many of them, but this one, Haraldskvaeði, was too grim for Aiden's tastes. He wouldn't like to imagine that, like in the poem, a Valkyrie and a raven might sit above them having idle conversations about the lives of the doomed warriors below. The thought of it gave him an itch right between his shoulder blades— the ephemeral irritation of being watched.

The sun was only barely rising when Arnnjorn gathered the men to leave. There was no shouting or great speeches. They couldn't risk their voices carrying over the hills to their enemy. In near silence, they moved out, creeping over the hills, intent not to disturb a single nesting bird. Aiden barely breathed as, far too soon for his liking, the enemy village came into view over the hill, looking so much like Arnnstead that he could almost have imagined they were home. They paused a moment before the last hill, knowing to move forward was to be exposed and forsake all chance of turning back. The men's eyes turned to Arnnjorn, who was looking at the village below them with cold disdain. Aiden searched instead for Einarr, never far from his side, and their eyes met in the pale early light. Einarr smiled at him reassuringly, and Aiden tried to smile back. Einarr seemed entirely unafraid. Why then was there a pit in Aiden's stomach, certain that something was about to go wrong?

"Are you ready to avenge me, men?" Arnnjorn called loudly, the time for stealth gone, raising his sword in the air above him to the shouts of his warriors. "Let no man go unpunished who was old enough to hold a weapon and did not raise it in defense of my sister! Go and seek glory!"

With a howl, Arnnjorn charged down the hill and into the village, and the men followed, carrying Aiden along with them like a terrible tide. Aiden clutched his axe and his shield, his heart beating so fast he could no longer feel it and was half-convinced it had stopped in fear. Still, he dared not run. To show cowardice now would be just as deadly as throwing himself on his enemy's spear. His only avenue of hope was forward.

They hit the village like a wave. The first people to stumble out of their homes in confusion at the noise were the first to be struck down. An instant later, they were followed by the more wary, their weapons brandished. But still, they were unprepared, scattered, and disorganized. Arnnjorn's men barreled through the streets in carefully organized chaos, the mounted men each leading a group of others, spreading them out quickly over the whole of the small village. Aiden, afraid but not panicked, lashed out at anyone who came at him. Aiden caught the axe blows of a furiously bellowing bearded man on his shield until the axe stuck and he could throw the man off, ducking under the man's reach to swing his own axe at the man's unprotected throat. The blood was hot and stank of metal, but Aiden couldn't allow it to turn his stomach. Not when there was another enemy coming, and another behind that, and another behind that...

He began to realize, something had gone wrong. The raid had gone on too long. His arms were weary and he couldn't see any of the mounted warriors meant to guide them. Now that the element of surprise was lost, the fight was more equal. Though Arnnjorn's men had dispatched a good number of the village warriors in the first rush, now the enemy had the advantage of fighting on their own territory. Strategy was mostly lost on Aiden, but he knew enough to see that this battle was quickly dissolving into chaos around him. Several buildings were on fire. Men wrestled on the ground, churned up and wet with blood until the mud made them indistinguishable from one another. Bodies were strewn haphazardly, no one making the effort to remove the wounded from the fray. The air was filled with sounds of pain and the roar of fire and the heavy sickly sweet stench of blood. Aiden, his shield held close, hurried through the streets, scanning the faces for Einarr, or even just someone he recognized who could tell him what was happening and what he was meant to do now. Their biggest advantage had been organization. How had that dissolved like this? What had gone wrong?

The worst of the fighting was still going on in the center of the town, and Aiden hovered at the edge of it, not yet prepared to throw himself back in. He heard one of the horses, screaming and struggling to get away, its reins tangled in the fallen beam of a burning house. He spotted Einarr's horse too, dead, nearly hidden in the mud. Einarr was not with it, though Aiden's heart wrenched like it was, panic beginning to rise like bile in his throat. Then he heard a shout he recognized too well, his heart leaping.

He rushed into the fray, swinging at anything that came too close, keeping his shield high as he pushed through, seeking out that shout. He found them at the very center. Arnnjorn knelt in the mud like a mountain fallen, grievously wounded. Einarr stood before him, defending his uncle, locked in combat with another warrior.

The stranger was taller than Einarr by a few inches, but built thinner and rangier. His hair was black as a raven's wing, long and ragged. On second glance, Aiden realized he didn't look much like the other villagers at all. His clothes were different, older and more worn. Everything about him had the mark of wildness, especially the way he swung at Einarr. He had stolen Arnnjorn's sword and flew at Einarr with it like a man possessed, terrifying rage in his every mad swing, screaming as he threw himself forward, ignoring everything else. It was clear Einarr was his only quarry. Einarr held him off, pushing the other man back for every step he took forward, matching him blow for blow. And yet, Aiden sensed he was holding back, defending but hesitating to make the killing blow. Why were his eyes so unsure? The madman's swings were wide open, so why wasn't Einarr finishing this? If he kept putting it off...

Aiden's breath stopped in his lungs as he saw Einarr's foot slip in the mud. Victory flashed in the dark-haired warrior's eyes as Einarr lost his balance, his guard dropping. But Aiden was already moving forward. Time slowed, his feet dragging in the mud, the seconds stretching out into a hateful eternity as he watched the sword coming down, reflected in Einarr's staring eyes. A shout was burning in his lungs, a wordless cry of refusal. He couldn't let it happen. He wouldn't! Any Valkyrie listening would hear Aiden screaming that it wasn't their time yet. Whatever the gods had planned, Aiden had decided they still had many years together, and he refused to allow any other outcome!

The madman's blow hit Aiden's shield so hard that Aiden's arm went numb, the shield splitting from the sheer force of the impact, the wood only holding together by the metal that braced it.

"Aiden!"

Aiden heard Einarr gasp his name behind him, but he couldn't look away from the stunned and wild eyes of the man in front of him, their color the black of space between the stars. The shock that had filled them briefly vanished like a spark in the night replaced with fiery fury as he wrenched his sword from Aiden's broken shield and swung it again. Aiden braced himself to move under the strike and lash at the man with his axe, but an arm around his waist stopped him.

Einarr had grabbed him, rolling them both out of the way. The dark-haired warrior's blow hit nothing but mud. Aiden scrambled back to his feet, dragging Einarr up with him. The mad warrior was staring at them in confusion as Einarr, gripping his sword, stepped in front of Aiden defensively. Sudden understanding dawned in that dark gaze, and he locked eyes with Aiden, staring right past Einarr with a smile that was all snarl and teeth.

"Grímr, no," Einarr was shouting, trying to block the stranger's view. "Your fight is with me!"

Aiden didn't know what was happening; all he knew was that he couldn't let Einarr fight this man alone.

As the dark-haired warrior rushed them again, Einarr stepped forward to return the blow, and Aiden was beside him. The other fighters had begun to take notice of them again, and Aiden guarded Einarr's back as he concentrated on the madman. But Aiden could see the fight had changed. The stranger kept lashing out past Einarr, ignoring opportunities to hurt the man in favor of striking out at Aiden instead. Aiden barely evaded his wild strikes again and again. And yet still Einarr seemed to be hesitating to take these opportunities to finish the fight. Why wouldn't he kill this stranger?

"Aiden!" Einarr cried as he caught the stranger's blade on his own and held it. "Run!"

"Never!" Aiden shouted back and, tired of whatever game Einarr was playing, darted under their held swords to bash the mad warrior in the chin with his broken shield and bury his axe in the man's shoulder. He'd aimed for the throat and missed, but knew it would be wound enough to drive the stranger off.

Sure enough, the stranger stumbled back and Aiden shifted to disengage, only to find his axe stuck, lodged in the man's collarbone. He felt a flicker of panic, released the axe at once, but it was too late. The dark-haired warrior's arm snapped around Aiden's waist like an iron bar, dragging him closer. Aiden twisted to get free, but the man was already moving, hauling him backwards toward the trapped horse. Aiden kicked at the man's legs, slapped at the axe wound in his shoulder, but the wild-eyed stranger seemed to feel no pain, ignoring Aiden's struggles entirely as he slashed at the reins keeping the horse trapped. Aiden twisted to pin Einarr with a wild eye, the other warrior frozen, unable to strike for fear of hitting his lover. Einarr could only watch as the stranger swung himself onto the horse with the still wildly struggling Aiden. The last thing Aiden saw before the pommel of the stranger's sword knocked the sense from his head was a crowd of enemies rising behind Einarr as the warrior stared after him in paralyzed horror.

Chapter Five

Motion woke Aiden. For a moment, he thought he was on a boat, and then realized the way his head was swimming was due to being hit, not the sea. Though he was moving, it was not the steady rock of waves, but the irregular, bouncing gait of a horse which he'd been thrown across the back of, strapped to the saddle like so much cargo. Gradually, a piece at a time, he put together what had happened, his aching head clearing as he regathered his scattered thoughts. He remembered the raid on Ingifast, Arnnjorn injured, and Einarr, locked in combat with a stranger he wouldn't kill. His vision was beginning to clear, though the motion of the horse made it all the harder to focus on anything before him. Grass slid by a few feet below his face, the occasional glimpse of the horse's hooves, a man's booted leg. He craned, pulling against his bonds, to follow that leg up to a face he could recognize. He was hardly surprised when he saw the stranger, his jaw set and his eyes cold. Einarr had called him Grímr. Aiden wondered uneasily how Einarr knew this sharp-featured stranger. More pressingly, he wondered why Grímr had captured him rather than killing him. Aiden couldn't imagine it was for any good purpose.

They were riding across a gray, rocky heath; dense shrubs tangling around bare stone outcroppings tumbled from the mountain above them, the slate dark gray and damp with early morning moisture. They jutted from the green pasture like so many gravestones, decorated by sweeps and flourishes of bright wildflowers. The sky was still dull, the sun not fully risen, and the air was cool against Aiden's skin. They must have ridden through the night, he realized.

He tested the ropes binding him. Wrists and ankles, strapped to the horse. If he tried to roll off, he'd be trampled. But if he could work his hands loose, get the stranger's knife, and kill him, he'd have all the time he needed to cut himself free. He began rolling and twisting his wrists as quietly as he could, trying to loosen the ropes. He eyed the man's back, contemplating how to get his knife from him, and found himself again wondering why Einarr hadn't killed him. There had been so many chances. Einarr must have had a reason. That was all Aiden could figure. He felt suddenly wary about killing the man when he didn't know what that reason was. He kept working at his ropes as he contemplated what to do. Maybe he could just threaten Grímr with the knife. But if it came down to it, he would definitely kill this stranger in order to get away. He'd just have to apologize to Einarr for it later.

The ropes around his wrists were steadily loosening. Aiden tried not to move too much, worried he would draw the stranger's attention at this late stage. He just needed a little more, and...

He inhaled sharply in victory as he pulled a hand free of the ropes, and he felt Grímr shift in response to the noise. Realizing he would have to move fast, Aiden dove for the knife in the other man's belt, shaking the rope off of his other hand. But he wasn't fast enough. Grímr caught him by the wrist, turning in his saddle, trying to keep one hand on the reins while he wrestled with Aiden, who was already scrabbling for the knife with his free hand. The stranger said nothing as they struggled, baring his teeth like an animal. Aiden wondered if the man could speak at all.

He gave a shout as he succeeded in getting the knife out of Grímr's belt, and in response, the stranger backhanded him hard. Aiden, still clutching the small knife, tumbled off the back of the horse and onto the rocky ground. Grit bit into his skin and tore as the rope around his still-bound feet dragged him behind the now panicked and galloping horse. Aiden scrambled to cut the rope tying him to the horse. Between the dirt flying at his face and the bouncing confusion throwing him this way and that, Aiden caught glimpses of Grímr trying to bring the horse back under control.

At last, the knife sliced through the rope and Aiden tumbled away, every bone in his body screaming pain from the rough treatment, but none so much as his right leg, which he was fairly certain the horse's hoof had come down on at least once. Still, dizzy and confused, he sat up to hack away the binding still around his ankle. A dozen yards away, Grímr had successfully regained control of the horse and was turning it around to face Aiden. He dismounted when he saw Aiden, dirty and bloodied, still on the ground, but within a few steps. Aiden had freed himself and was getting to his feet, clawing at the rocky dirt as he tried to run before he even had his legs under him. His right leg screamed in pain every time he put weight on it, but Aiden, gasping in agony, ran on it anyway, scrambling up a broken stony hill to get away. Hopefully, whatever purpose Grímr had in keeping him was unimportant, and the stranger wouldn't bother to chase him. He realized that hope had been naive as he felt a hand snag the collar of his shirt and yank him backwards, his leg twisting painfully. He cried out, turned to aim a wild punch at the man and felt it connect, a moment before he was hit back so hard, consciousness almost fled him again, leaving him staggered and stumbling before Grímr grabbed him by the shirt. The stranger slammed him against one of the hill's larger rocky outcroppings, the impact knocking the knife from his hand. The wall of stone grated against Aiden's cheek as the other man pressed against him. Grímr's body, crushing him against the stone, was longer and leaner than Einarr's, but just as firm and unrelenting, holding Aiden in place despite how he struggled. He went still as he felt the cold point of a blade against his throat.

"Listen to me," Grímr spoke in a voice like gravel, low and rough, the first words Aiden had heard him speak. "I'd rather keep you alive, but it won't disrupt my plans that much to just kill you if you cause me too much trouble."

He pressed closer, his knee sliding between Aiden's thighs. Aiden could feel the other man against every inch of him, and he shivered, suddenly worried for more than just his life.

44

"It would serve my purposes only a little less well to defile you and gut you and leave you on this hill for him to find." Grímr's mouth moved against Aiden's ear, lips brushing his skin, his breath hot. "So consider yourself lucky that I'd rather have you alive, and stop tempting me to change my plans."

Deciding not to press his luck, Aiden swallowed his pride and relaxed, ceasing his struggling. He wanted his chance to kill this man, and he wouldn't get it if he acted too recklessly.

"Good boy," Grímr said in approval as Aiden softened against him. "Resist the urge to do something stupid, and you'll live a long time yet."

He backed away, letting Aiden breathe again, and pulled the smaller man's hands behind his back, retying them with an impatient grumble. Once they were tied, he pulled Aiden away from the wall and shoved him toward the horse, but Aiden had only taken a step before his injured leg buckled under him. He bit his lip to stifle a cry of pain as fire seemed to shoot up through the bone.

"Get up," Grímr demanded, suspicious, but when Aiden tried, the leg only gave out again. Running on it through adrenaline-powered fear had made the pain worse, and now it couldn't bear his weight at all. Grímr huffed in annoyance and grabbed Aiden by the arm, dragging him up onto his feet and holding him there as Aiden limped toward the horse. Aiden felt a rush of hot shame at having to rely on the stranger. He wasn't going to be running away on a leg like this. He'd either have to steal the horse, or else hope someone else came to rescue him. He looked back at the way they'd come, hoping he might see Einarr's silhouette on the heath. But there was no one. Aiden had no way of knowing if the man had even escaped the battle alive. He might already be dead. The thought caused a cold pit of grief in Aiden's stomach. He didn't believe it— he couldn't. He would know if Einarr was dead; he'd be able to feel it somehow. The other man was definitely alive, and on his way here now to rescue Aiden. Aiden could afford to believe nothing else.

Grímr tied Aiden to the saddle again, but allowed him to sit up this time at least, riding properly instead of over the back like luggage. The only problem was that he placed Aiden in front of him. Aiden rode hunched over to avoid Grímr's chest pressing against his back, but he couldn't avoid the arms that caged him any more than he could ignore the way his leg throbbed in pain every time the horse's uneven steps jostled it, which seemed to be nearly every other step. The pain was enough to make him dizzy, and he struggled to focus past it and stay awake.

"So, why are you doing this, anyway?" Aiden asked as they rode, needing something to focus on besides the pain. "Einarr seemed to know you."

"If he hasn't told you about me, perhaps you're less important to him than I thought you were." Grímr didn't look away from the horizon as he spoke, clearly unconcerned with Aiden. He scowled as something occurred to him, lip curling in disgust.

"Or maybe he really is the kind of scum who could forget a thing like that," he said.

"Einarr isn't scum." Aiden's hackles raised defensively, though letting his heart beat faster only made the pain throbbing in his leg worse, the black creeping at the edges of his vision a little darker. "Einarr is the most honorable man I've ever met. He remembered you, or else he would have killed you ten times over, just in the part of your fight I saw. He was holding back to spare you."

"Then he's become an idiot," Grímr hissed. "Because I would not hold back to spare him. If he doesn't realize by now what he is to me—"

Grímr suddenly cut himself off, looking away.

"I've been in the wilds too long," he grumbled. "I've forgotten what it's like to talk with someone."

"You're an outlaw," Aiden realized, shaking his head to try and clear it, "Aren't you?"

Grímr didn't answer. Outlawry was one of the harshest punishments Norse justice could dispense, reserved only for the most serious of crimes. Cowardice, assaulting a woman, and treason, among others, were the crimes for which a man could be made an outlaw. His property would be stripped from him, and he would be banished from civilization, with all men forbidden from offering him aid or shelter of any kind. In addition, all legal protections were denied him, meaning any man could kill him with no repercussions. Many did not survive long, freezing or starving without supplies or shelter. Most outlaws did not live past their first day, when whatever enemy they'd angered to get themselves outlawed came looking for revenge. The few that did survive became hard and cold, criminals and bandits. Exactly the kind to attack an unarmed woman on the road. Aiden wondered if Grímr hadn't orchestrated this raid for some reason.

"So, where are you taking me?" Aiden asked. "What exactly are you planning to do with me?"

Again, Grímr said nothing, ignoring Aiden's question entirely. They hit a particularly nasty bump, and Aiden's vision swam.

"Hey, answer me," Aiden demanded, his words slurring as his head bobbed. "I deserve to know."

Still, Grímr was silent, only catching Aiden's shoulder as they hit another bump and Aiden couldn't keep back a pained groan. He couldn't keep his thoughts straight.

"Where are we going?" he asked again, insisting on answers. "Where are we..."

His head thumped against Grímr's chest as he passed out, the pain and exhaustion finally overwhelming him. The world went black.

Chapter Six

When he woke again, it was evening and he was laying on his back, the stars wheeling past a blue black sky above him while a fire crackled to his left. His hands were tied in front of him and, most distressingly, he realized he'd been undressed, left in nothing but his smallclothes. He sat up quickly, though his head protested the sudden movement, shivering in the chilly night air. Grímr was sitting near him by the low fire, cooking a scrawny rabbit.

"What did you do to me?" Aiden demanded, skin prickling with distress.

"Pass out with questions, wake with questions," Grímr grumbled. "Is that the only way you know how to speak?"

"Why am I naked?" Aiden insisted, ready to attack the man if he didn't get an answer soon, and damn the consequences.

"Relax." The man rolled his eyes and reached behind him to grab a bundle of clothing, throwing it to Aiden. "Your virtue is intact, milady."

Aiden caught the clothing as Grímr gave a mock bow. Aiden saw it was his own things, neatly put away.

"I had to take off your lower half to tend your leg," Grímr explained, indicating Aiden's right calf, which he now saw had been set and splinted. He could see the ugly bruises, blue-black as the sky, peeking out around the edges of the bandages. The horse had done a number on him.

49

"You were feverish from the pain," Grímr went on. "The cold brought it and the swelling down. I've no interest in scrawny English thralls."

"I'm not a thrall," Aiden snapped at once, forgetting his brief gratitude. "I'm a free man."

"No interest in scrawny English free men, either," Grímr replied, unfazed, "Now if you want any of this rabbit, you'll learn silence for a few minutes."

Aiden hadn't eaten since the morning before, and the smell of the rabbit cooking had his mouth watering already, so he fell quiet, considering the man in front of him. He hunched over his fire like a wild dog guarding his prey. There was much of the wild dog about him, in fact— all sharp angles and scruffy, ragged edges. With how long he must have been alone, taking care of no one but himself, Aiden was hardly surprised that he was a little wild. Aiden continued to watch him, half in wariness and half in curiosity as he struggled to dress himself with bound hands. He managed to get his pants on, but found himself stumped for how to get into his shirt. He put it aside after a moment in frustration, though he was starting to shake from the cold, which would only get worse as the night deepened.

"So, when will you tell me how you know Einarr?" he asked, growing impatient. "Do you have some sort of grudge against him?"

"More questions!" Grímr, annoyed, stabbed the stick he'd been using to turn the coals down into the dirt beside him. "You're like a twittering bird! Do you never stop?"

"I stop when I learn what I'm after," Aiden answered, kicking at the rocks in front of him in frustration, sending a spray of them at Grímr. "So tell me already, and I'll be quiet!"

Grímr shielded himself from the rocks with an arm, then darted forward with a snarl, surprising Aiden, who couldn't scurry backwards fast enough to avoid Grímr's hand closing around his throat, shoving him down into the dirt to lean over him, teeth bared like he was thinking of taking a bite out of the other man. Aiden stared up him in wide-eyed shock, caught off guard by the sudden escalation.

"Why don't you answer a question for me, instead?" Grímr growled, gripping Aiden's throat tightly enough to make his eyes water. "You were a thrall, weren't you? No Englishman lives on these coasts out of chains. But there's no collar on you now. So, how did you buy your freedom, little bird? What did you sell to buy yourself back?"

The hand not around Aiden's throat grabbed Aiden roughly between his legs, instead. Aiden tensed, electric fear running through him, unable to even gasp as he scrabbled at the hand clutching his throat.

"Why did Einarr fight so much harder when you were beside him?" Grímr demanded, staring directly into Aiden's eyes as the smaller man struggled to breathe. "Who does this part of you belong to?"

Aiden struggled, kicking at Grímr's legs in instinctual panic, but Grímr only scoffed, letting go of Aiden abruptly, throwing him back onto the rocky ground as he moved away, returning to his rabbit like

51

nothing had happened. Aiden lay where he'd been left, coughing as he tried to regain his breath, rolling onto his side so that Grímr wouldn't see his face. Shame burned through him like fever, bringing hot, angry tears to his eyes, outraged and embarrassed that Grímr had accused him of such things and had touched him that way. He knew it wasn't unusual for thralls, male and female, to offer themselves like that for money, but Aiden never had. He'd earned his freedom fighting to defend his village and the people he loved. But he doubted Grímr would believe that. It was clear what kind of opinion Grímr had of him, and Aiden didn't think the other man was worth the effort of convincing otherwise. He lay where he was, the red curls of his hair falling across his face as he focused on taking deep breaths, shivering with shame and the cold.

"Get up."

Aiden flinched at the order, sitting up enough to eye Grímr suspiciously. The dark-haired man had moved near him again, holding a curved knife out threateningly.

"Get up," he repeated. "Hold out your hands."

Aiden, eyeing that knife warily, did as he was told, wincing as his leg complained at the movement, and finally offered his bound wrists. Grímr began untying them in rough tugs.

"Put on your shirt," he said as he finished. "Make a move I don't like, and I'll gut you like a fish, understand?"

Aiden rubbed his raw, reddened wrists and nodded in terse agreement, reaching for his shirt, which he pulled over his head with some relief as the thick blue wool stopped the night breeze at once. He ran his fingers over the embroidery at the hem as he tugged it down. This shirt had been a gift from Einarr— one of the first things the other man had ever given him. It matched the sky blue bead in his hair, which he'd also received from the other man.

"I know that tunic," Grímr said thoughtfully, looking at it. "That was Bard's."

Aiden eyed the other man in wary surprise. He'd known Einarr's brother?

"I guess the idiot must have died, if they're giving his things to thralls now," Grímr muttered, and turned back to the rabbit to take it off the fire. Aiden wanted to protest again that he wasn't a thrall, but he swallowed his annoyance instead. He wouldn't waste his words on a man with no honor.

"Did I finally figure out how to keep you quiet, little bird?" Grímr asked with a bitter laugh. "Just when I was getting used to your incessant twittering. Here."

Aiden, refusing to look at the other man, was caught by surprise when Grímr shoved a portion of the rabbit into his hands, the grease of the brown, crispy skin burning his fingers. He pulled the sleeve of his shirt down over his hand to protect it, and Grímr snorted with laughter again.

"Old Bard would have had a fit," he said in cruel amusement. "Eat it before it gets cold. When I'm

53

finished, I'll be tying your hands again whether you've finished or not."

He turned to his own portion, eating with all the grace of a starving animal. Realizing he wouldn't have long, Aiden hurried to eat his own portion as well. Hungry as he was, it tasted delicious. Part of him wondered why Grímr was bothering to feed him when Aiden obviously meant so little to him. The rest of him was just grateful. He couldn't figure Grímr out. One moment, he was threatening him with death and worse, the next, he was tending Aiden's wounds, feeding him, and keeping him warm. What was this man's purpose? He needed Aiden alive and healthy, but what for?

Grímr kept his promise, tying Aiden back up again the moment he finished eating. What Aiden didn't expect was to be pushed down onto his face while Grímr tied his wrists behind his back, then fastened them by a short length of rope to the ankle of his uninjured leg.

"You didn't think I'd leave you with just your hands tied, did you?" Grímr said with a laugh. "I intend to get some sleep tonight."

The length of rope between Aiden's wrists and ankle was long enough that it wasn't pulled taught, but he was sure it would get uncomfortable before morning. He struggled against it in annoyance, hoping he could find a way out of it. Grímr watched him squirm with a wolfish grin.

"That look suits you, little bird," he teased as Aiden ended up on his back, panting and red-faced as his injured leg throbbed. "I can see why Einarr took a liking to you in chains. But I think a cage would suit a songbird like you better. Maybe that's what I'll do with you when we get where we're going."

"And where is that, exactly?" Aiden, hurting and irritated, gave up on his brief and stubborn silence.

"Not sure yet." Grímr stood with a sigh and a stretch. "Just going. To the coast, perhaps. Take a ship out of this country. All that matters to me is that we go far enough that Einarr never finds you."

"If this is about him," Aiden started, twisting in his ropes with frustration, "Why are you bothering with me?"

"Because he cares about you." Grímr's voice dropped low and threatening, warning Aiden that he was touching on a topic the other man didn't feel like explaining, "And I'd rather have him alive and suffering than dead."

"Then why not just kill me?" Aiden huffed, in too much pain and anger to care at this point. "Why feed me and bring me with you when you could just dump my body at his feet? Do you even know why you're doing this?"

"Oh, delivering your body to him is still an option, don't think it isn't," Grímr snarled, "But it isn't enough for what he deserves, not nearly. No, I want him knowing you're out there somewhere, not knowing what happened to you, but knowing it's his fault, and that he'll never see you again. Maybe after a few years, once the pain has started to dull, I'll cut out an eye or a finger and send it to him, just so that he knows you're still alive, still suffering because of him."

"Years?" Aiden repeated, fear beginning to creep in his veins at the thought of this madman cutting on him for years. "You really intend to keep this up that long? What could he have possibly done that you'd spend so much time just to hurt him?"

Grímr's face twitched with anger as he remembered, and he looked at Aiden with a sudden flash of anger like he was considering strangling him again. Aiden curled up defensively, heart racing. Grímr huffed.

"He really didn't tell you," the dark-haired man said in disgust. "Do you know anything about his history? If he didn't even tell you about that, how can I be sure he'll even care about you enough to come after you?"

That stung more than Aiden cared to admit. He bit his tongue, turning his face away from Grímr's.

"Maybe, if he catches up to us, I'll have him tell you." Grímr lay down beside the fire with a ragged fur and closed his eyes. "If he doesn't care enough to chase us, then it hardly matters. I'll just kill you and try again."

Aiden shuddered and didn't respond, and soon, he heard Grímr's breathing even out in sleep. He went back to tugging on his ropes, struggling to get loose, or at least more comfortable. He stayed at it for hours, but in the end, he only wore himself out and rubbed his wrists till they bled. His broken leg wasn't appreciating all the moving around, either. At last, as the sky was graying with dawn, he gave up and fell asleep, exhausted.

Chapter Seven

He was woken less than an hour later, the sky still pale and grim above him, when he felt someone touching his hands. He jerked away, then realized it was Grímr, untying him and muttering in annoyance.

"Do you think bandages grow on trees?" he growled. "Do you think I can just walk into town and buy them? I have to make them or steal them, neither of which I have time for right now."

"Sorry," Aiden said reflexively, still tired and groggy. Grímr only huffed in response, throwing down the ropes. Aiden slowly unfolded himself from the uncomfortable posture he'd been in all night, groaning as his stiff joints complained. Now that his hands were in front of him again, he could see how raw and bloody they were. Those marks wouldn't be going away for a while.

Grímr appeared in front of him again, startling Aiden as he grabbed the smaller man's hands and began pouring water over his wrists, rinsing out the grit and fibers from the ropes. He was still muttering in irritation, but his touch was careful and thorough as he cleaned the injury and bandaged it. Aiden, surprised by the attention and still not completely awake, didn't resist. This was the first time he'd been this close to Grímr when they weren't fighting. He noticed, though Grímr had been careful to tend all of Aiden's injuries, the axe wound in the warrior's own shoulder seemed to have been ignored. It was a matted mess of dried blood and his own torn clothing now, certain to get infected if he didn't deal with it soon. Aiden wondered why the other man would ignore it.

"Thank you." Aiden withdrew his hands as Grímr finished, his thoughts full of questions.

"Don't thank me!" Grímr snapped, "Don't apologize, either. Just stop hurting yourself. That's my job."

"How reassuring."

Grímr only glared at him and, shocking no one, tied Aiden up again, fixing the other end to the horse's saddle while he kicked dirt over the embers of the fire, not trying hard at all to hide it. Presumably, he wanted Einarr to be able to follow them, either for the sake of keeping his enemy in suspense longer, or in hopes of an eventual confrontation.

Once the fire was out, Grímr turned to Aiden, surprising the younger man as he suddenly grabbed Aiden by the waist. With relatively little effort, he lifted Aiden up on to the horse, only wincing once as the movement tugged on the wound in his shoulder. Aiden would have thought such an injury would be searingly painful. And yet, Grímr continued to ignore it as though it were a mere scratch. How could he just keep going like this?

He swung up on to the horse behind Aiden, and they set out just as the sun was beginning to properly rise over the hills. Their path took them through a bleak valley— all tumbled gray stone and barren slopes— but in this early hour, even it was lovely in its lonesome way. The sun was burning off the iridescent mist from the broken slate, illuminating the tops of the mountains in golden light and casting the lee in deep purple shadow. Through the lingering, low morning cloud that trailed river-like through the bottom of the valley, their horse proceeded like a funeral ship, his head the proud prow splitting the silver current for the hunched, cold figures on his back. Aiden gazed upwards toward those golden slopes, where hardy spring flowers, white as stars, blanketed the earth like late snow banks, drifting in the breeze. But Grímr never looked anywhere but directly ahead, his attention turned ever inward to his own unhappy thoughts.

"So, how long have you been an outlaw?" Aiden asked when the silence grew like a lake too deep for him to ford.

"I wondered when you'd start on the questions again." Grímr barely even sounded annoyed anymore, just resigned to Aiden's insistent company.

"You've spent too long alone." Aiden looked back at Grímr with a serious frown. "Normal people prefer conversation to just sitting around silently."

"You would know what's normal," Grímr scoffed, "An argr thrall. An *English* argr thrall."

"You're as wrong about all three of those things as you are about everything else." Aiden's lip curled in anger and irritation at being called that again. "And I spent long enough alone to get my fill of silence. You've probably been alone longer than I have, so stop being stubborn and answer the question."

"Ask your master if he catches us." Grímr urged the horse on, and Aiden could feel the arms on either side of him flexing, tensing with annoyance. "It's his doing that I was outlawed in the first place. Not that he cared then or now. He'll care before I'm done with him, I can tell you that much."

"What exactly did he do?" Aiden bit the inside of his cheek, becoming tired of Grímr's habit of badmouthing the man Aiden loved while supplying no actual reasons for his dislike. "You still haven't told me."

"Maybe I don't feel like talking about it." Grímr glared down at Aiden angrily enough to make Aiden feel briefly cowed. "But perhaps you'd care to lead the conversation. You could tell me about how you were captured and became a thrall. That should be an entertaining story to pass the time, yes? Tell me, did Einarr kill your family before or after he took you?"

"Enough!" Aiden leaned away from Grímr, nearly unbalancing himself from the horse in his haste to get away from the man and those incredibly unhappy memories. "Your point is made! I won't ask any more."

Grímr spat toward the ground, his expression sour.

"Finally."

Aiden let the silence linger a while longer. The sun climbed higher, light spilling down into the valley and chasing the last of the chill from its depths. Aiden, still sore from his uncomfortable night, relished the warmth on his aching muscles. What he wouldn't give for a bath in the hot spring above the village right now. Or to wash at all. He hadn't grown up washing every day the way the Northmen did, but he'd become quite used to it in his time with them. Going without it now left him feeling grimy and unpleasant. Grímr looked well-kept in spite of his ragged nature; Aiden had to assume he bathed normally, and was choosing not to waste the time on it now for some reason Aiden couldn't fathom.

He spotted a glimmer of light reflecting on water on the slopes ahead of them and felt a flicker of excitement.

"Hey," he said, continuing when Grímr grunted in acknowledgement, "It looks like there's a spring ahead. We could stop and wash."

"We don't stop," Grímr replied at once, unfazed.

"You smell awful," Aiden countered, bristling at the out of hand dismissal. "If I'm going to have to be tied to you for the foreseeable future, you could at least do me the courtesy of not smothering me with your stench. Not to mention that wound on your shoulder is going sour. I can smell it from here. If you don't wash it out soon, it'll become rancid, and it'll be me and your corpse who meet Einarr when he catches up."

Grímr gave a wordless snarl of annoyance at Aiden's tirade and yanked on the reins, turning the horse toward the glimmer of water.

"Fine! We'll wash. Are you happy, little bird? If all prisoners are as demanding as you, I can't see how any are ever kept alive more than a day!"

62

Aiden smiled, relieved he had managed to convince the man of this much, at least. It took another hour or so for the horse to make it over the craggy hillside to the spring Aiden had spotted. It was a small, relatively shallow pool collected in a depression in the stony mountain slope, the water blue-green as a jewel and steaming slightly in the cool air.

Grímr slid off the horse first and looped its reins around a stone, then lifted Aiden off as easily as if he was a child. Setting him down, Grímr untied Aiden's hands, then stepped back.

"Undress," he ordered.

Aiden balked at the unexpectedly direct order, blushing.

"What?" Grímr wrinkled his nose at Aiden's shocked expression. "Did you expect to bathe fully-clothed? Besides, you're less likely to run off if you're naked. Now, undress."

Aiden, still slightly uncomfortable, but realizing the other man had a point, did as he was told. Uncomfortably aware of Grímr's eyes on him, Aiden stripped while the other man watched in silence.

"Toss me your clothes," Grímr ordered next, showing no sign of being phased by Aiden's body. Aiden reluctantly obeyed, and Grímr gestured for him to get into the water.

"Don't get your bandages wet," the older man ordered. "I don't have much left, and I don't care to replace them."

Aiden assumed the man meant his wrists. There wasn't much he could do about the bandages on his injured leg, which he eased into the water first, sighing happily as the warm water soaked into his muscles. He slid in after it with a groan of relief, almost forgetting about Grímr entirely until he heard the shuffle of clothing and looked up to see Grímr peeling off his own clothing. He winced sympathetically as the other man's shirt, stiff with blood, stuck to his injury, pulling at it in a way that had to be painful, though Grímr barely seemed to react, even as the loss of the matted fabric holding it together caused the wound to reopen and ooze sluggishly. Grímr ignored it, discarding his clothes and climbing in beside Aiden.

Aiden was briefly stunned by the sight of the other man. He was handsome, certainly, but that wasn't what caught Aiden's attention. The man was too thin, muscle taught beneath his skin, clearly only just getting enough to eat to maintain himself, and not always that. And nearly every inch of him was riddled with scars. Wounds from bows, knives, spears, the claws of animals. Grímr's hide was a history of violence, overwritten again and again, a palimpsest of pain. Not even the hardest warriors of Einarr's village had so many scars. Grímr looked like he'd been through nothing less than hell and back. It sparked pity in Aiden that he resented and tried to push away, but couldn't quite dismiss. What sort of life must the man have lived to end up in that kind of state?

Aiden settled to washing himself, trying to dismiss his worry. It was pointless to worry about someone like Grímr, especially when Aiden was his prisoner, and currently dependent on him thanks to his broken leg. Still, he found his eyes returning to the other man as they washed themselves. The wound on Grímr's shoulder, which Aiden had given him, looked as ugly as any Aiden had ever seen, its edges an angry red with growing infection. That was a deadly wound if left untreated. But Grímr seemed content to splash water on it and ignore it. Aiden's worry grew. If this idiot did die out here, Aiden would not get far with his leg in this condition. He wouldn't be able to defend himself if animals or other outlaws attacked. He wouldn't even be able to find his own food. Would he survive long enough for Einarr to find him? He didn't dare allow himself to consider the possibility that Einarr might not be looking for him at all.

"You need to deal with that," he said at last, agitation reaching a boiling point. "Why are you ignoring it? Is all this talk of revenge only for show while you're looking for a way to die?"

"Be quiet." Grímr turned away from Aiden, focused on washing out his long, black hair. "I can tend my own wounds."

"Except you aren't," Aiden pointed out, crossing his arms over his chest. "You're just letting it fester. It's going to kill you."

"I've had worse. Haven't died yet."

"What a great reason to tempt the fates. At least clean it."

65

Grímr was silent for a moment, mouth working like he was actively resisting saying the words that were trying to force their way out anyway.

"Can't," he finally confessed.

"Why not?" Aiden moved closer, baffled.

"Hurts."

He turned further away from Aiden, as though he were ashamed of the admission, or wary that such an admission of weakness would lead to immediate ridicule or attack.

"Of course it hurts." Aiden stared at the man, mouth open in confusion. "I lodged a damn axe in your collarbone. I don't even know how you pulled the thing out alone."

"I'm good at ignoring pain," Grímr shrugged, and then looked like he regretted it.

"I can see that," Aiden snorted, not at all amused. "If it hurts so much, let me clean it for you."

Grímr turned to meet Aiden's eye, confused and suspicious.

"Why?"

"Because my leg is broken and I'll die out here without you," Aiden explained in the plainest terms possible. "I need you to stay alive long enough for Einarr to catch up and kill you."

Grímr grunted. Aiden wasn't sure if it was understanding or disappointment, but he turned to face Aiden again. His wet hair stuck to the handsome, aristocratic angles of his face and water beaded on his skin invitingly, reminding Aiden once again, distractingly, that a little better-fed and cleaned up,

Grímr would be an incredibly attractive man. He did his best to ignore that thought as he moved closer to reach the injured shoulder. Grímr offered him a bit of rag, and then turned his face away, presumably not wanting Aiden to see the pain in his expression as Aiden began cleaning the dried blood, grit, and fibers from the deep, ugly wound. It was nasty work, and soon the wound was bleeding again, which Aiden took for a good thing. Maybe it would clear out some of the impurities of infection.

"It needs to be stitched," he determined when he was done.

"Don't have the tools for it," Grímr replied, voice rough with pain. "Could burn it. That'd stop the bleeding."

Aiden shuddered at the thought.

"Maybe if we were in a village or I thought you were on the verge of bleeding to death," Aiden said, "But I've seen how fast burns can turn sour. In a village where we could keep it clean, it might save you, but out here, it'll kill you as surely as not treating the wound at all. We'll pack it and bandage it. Keep an eye on it until we can get supplies to stitch it."

"And when do you think that will be?" Grímr snorted. "For an outlaw and his prisoner? I can't just go into town and buy these things, little bird."

"We'll figure something out," Aiden declared. "Where do you keep your bandages?"

Grímr held out a hand to tell Aiden to stay where he was and climbed out of the spring to fetch the bandages, just strips of torn, clean fabric. He returned, sitting on the edge of the spring as Aiden carefully packed the wound with some of the fabric, then bound it closed with the rest.

"That should help a little," Aiden said as he wrapped bandages around Grímr's shoulder, feeling only a little doubtful. "I heard once that honey prevents infection. Maybe if we find some..."

"Aye, and I'm certain we'll find a needle and thread right beneath the comb as well," Grímr said sarcastically, "And then a healer will spring fully-formed from the hive."

"There's no reason to be nasty about it," Aiden grumbled. "I'm trying to help."

Grímr grunted wordlessly, and Aiden rolled his eyes.

It was difficult not to think about how close he was to the other man, both of them naked, clean skin wet and warm under his fingers. It was the best way to do this, but it still left him feeling unsteady and a touch uncomfortable. Grímr's hair, uncombed, was tangled and knotted in front of him, and Aiden couldn't help remembering Einarr's fingers running through his hair. How intimate and soothing it always felt to have the other man taking care of him that way. Why had he refused the last time? Such a petty thing to be angry about, really. He was insecure and anxious, but he shouldn't have let it come between them like that. If he never saw Einarr again, and he'd spoiled their last days together with that argument...

He shook his head to clear his thoughts and focus again on Grímr in front of him. He needed to figure out a way to deal with this man. He couldn't escape, he couldn't kill Grímr, and he couldn't allow him to die. He certainly couldn't allow the man to flee the country with him. The only option then was to somehow change Grímr's mind about what he was doing— which Aiden was certain he couldn't do If both Einarr and Grímr refused to tell him what had happened between them. So, step one had to be figuring out what Grímr was so stridently seeking revenge for. He chewed his lip as he considered how to make the other man open up.

"Einarr didn't kill my family, you know."

Grímr, who'd been looking away, lost in thought, looked back in mild confusion at Aiden's statement.

"You wanted to hear about how I was captured and made a thrall, didn't you?" Aiden asked, focusing on the bandages and not the unpleasant memories he was about to dredge up. "Well, the first thing you got wrong— Einarr never killed my family. They were already dead."

Grímr said nothing, neither silencing Aiden nor encouraging him. Considering how often the man told Aiden to be quiet, Aiden figured that was encouragement in itself.

"My mother was a pagan foreigner my father brought back from war," he continued. "She was already pregnant with me then. I can't even be certain he was my father, but I was most certainly a bastard. She died when I was a few young. He lived long enough to teach me how to tend the sheep, then he followed her and I was alone."

"Not an uncommon story," Grímr pointed out, and Aiden nodded, not offended. It *was* fairly common.

"Einarr's raiding party stopped in my village to trade for supplies before they headed home for the harvest," Aiden continued. "The village leaders tried to cheat them, so they came back and burned the village in the night. I fought, and it reminded Einarr of his brother, so he stopped the other men from killing me by saying he wanted me as a thrall."

"You must have been thrilled," Grímr chuckled, and Aiden's fingers slipped on the bandages, grazing the other man's chest. He pulled away quickly and tucked the end of the bandage in, finished.

"I was furious," he went on. "I fought him, tried to get away at every opportunity. But I'd been alone for a long time. And he was kind to me. Soon, I realized I was happier living in his house than I had ever been living alone. So, I stopped fighting. And when danger threatened Arnnstead, I fought with him to protect it, hard enough that I earned my freedom."

"You know," Aiden jumped in surprise as he felt Grímr's hand at the small of his back, pulling him closer. "I've been alone a long time too. No one's been kind to me in a long while."

Aiden flushed scarlet and quickly pushed the other man away, squirming to get out of his grip. The outlaw's skin was hot against his own, slick with moisture. Grímr didn't try to hold on to him, letting Aiden flee to the other side of the little pool. Aiden's heart raced, suddenly feeling unsafe, watching Grímr with the wary eyes of an animal.

"I wouldn't treat you badly, you know," Grímr argued. "Better than Einarr, I bet."

"No, thank you," Aiden said sharply, not looking at Grímr, who eventually sighed and stood, leaving the spring behind and going back to his clothes.

"Get dressed," he ordered. "We've lingered here long enough."

Aiden scrubbed his face quickly, still feeling uneasy, then did as he was told, dressing himself with a little difficulty, his splinted leg making pants a trial. But like hell would he be going without them after that.

Back on the horse, a new uncomfortable silence reigned, which Aiden found himself reluctant to break. He'd been propositioned like that once or twice before, usually by very drunk men in Arnnstead. The first time, Aiden hadn't been sure how he was allowed to respond, but Einarr had set the man straight and made it clear to Aiden that, now that he was no longer a thrall, he was under no obligation to agree to such things. The second time, Aiden had dealt with the situation himself. This time, however, he couldn't deal with the situation by just decking Grímr and leaving. It left him unsure what was the wisest way to respond, and paralyzingly aware of every move Grímr made. Every time the other man shifted or his chest brushed Aiden's back as Aiden sat before him on the horse, Aiden's heart would skip a beat, his skin tingling and his hair raising.

"You know," Grímr broke the silence, his breath warm on the back of Aiden's neck, making him tense in surprise, "Einarr probably planned to raid your village from the beginning. They didn't come into the village to trade. They were just seeing what you had worth taking."

"You don't know what you're talking about," Aiden responded at once, turning his head away and hunching his shoulders to try and avoid the touch of the other man's breath on his skin.

"I know better than you," Grímr pointed out. "I was born here. I've been a Viking with your Einarr. I bet he knew what he was going to do to you the moment he set foot in that village and saw you. He probably set it up to make you think he was rescuing you. Get him on your good side to make getting what he wanted from you easier."

Aiden grit his teeth, wishing he could reach back and slap the other man.

"It wasn't like that." Aiden trembled with anger and with worry at how plausible what Grímr was saying sounded. "I'm not an idiot. I would know if he used me that way. More importantly, Einarr isn't that kind of man. He's honest and honorable and brave. I've never met a man better than him."

Grímr scoffed, his lip curling in disgust.

"You only see of him what he wants to show you," Grímr said, bristling. "He still hides all his feelings behind that smile, doesn't he? Do you think you're the first English boy he's taken a shine to?"

Aiden felt those words like a knife, unable to help the way his thoughts ran away, imagining Einarr bringing home other men. He hadn't been under any illusion that he'd been Einarr's first, but somehow, the way Grímr put it had him imagining Einarr lurking around foreign villages, picking out young men to toy with. The thought made his stomach turn. It wasn't in character for Einarr at all. He definitely would never do something like that. At least, as far as Aiden knew. But once again, the thought came creeping of how little Aiden really knew Einarr.

"It's your turn to talk," Aiden said suddenly, his posture stiff and his voice cold. "I told you about how I was captured. Now you tell me what Einarr did to you."

He felt the other man grow still behind him, and for a long moment, they were both silent. Aiden wondered if the other man intended to reply at all.

"We grew up together," Grímr said eventually, "In Ingifast. Arnnjorn's brother, Einarr's father, was a mighty warrior, well respected. His mother was a wise woman and a healer. He was in an entirely different class from me. My father was bondi, a free man, but only a poor farmer. My mother was a freed thrall. I would never be Einarr's equal, but children don't think about such things. We were friends."

Aiden nodded, having expected this much. The kind of anger Aiden saw in Grímr's eyes only came from a bond broken. You couldn't hate a stranger the way you could hate someone who'd once been close to you. Saying nothing, he let Grímr continue. But

73

Grímr's expression had twisted into sour unhappiness at some memory.

"And then he proved it had never meant anything to him," Grímr ground out through clenched teeth. "And because of him, I was made an outlaw, while he went on to become his uncle's heir, unsullied by any of it."

"What happened?" Aiden asked, frowning. "What did he do?"

"The same thing he'll do to you if you let him," Grímr answered, looking down at Aiden with fire in his eyes. "So give up on him now, before you get hurt, and be mine instead."

Aiden flinched away at the offer, and then regretted it when he saw the flash of miserable frustration in Grímr's expression.

"Whatever happened," Aiden tried to insist, his heart hammering as he tried to defend Einarr, "It must have been some kind of mistake. A misunderstanding. Einarr's a good man. If he could have done anything, I know he would have. Especially for someone he cared about."

Grímr shook his head, looking away.

"I hate it," he muttered, "The way your eyes soften when you talk about him. I'd make you despise him if I could."

Aiden's face heated and he turned away, facing forward again in embarrassment.

"I would treat you better than him," Grímr promised again, and Aiden's breath caught as the other man leaned closer to bear over him, lips brushing the back of his neck, a free hand squeezing his hip. "I would love you more truly. That man doesn't know the meaning of the word."

"You don't love me," Aiden said, breathless and tense as Grímr pulled Aiden's hips back more firmly against his own. "You just want to take me from him. I won't be part of that."

"I could love you." Grímr was pressing kisses to Aiden's throat, his hand wandering over the younger man's stomach. "A boy like you is easy to love. Let me show you."

"I won't," Aiden sat stiffly, ignoring the other man's touch as best as he could, struggling not to respond. "I won't do what you want."

"Why not?" Grímr's hands grew more demanding, his hand moving to Aiden's sensitive chest, every step of the horse below them rocking his hips against Aiden's backside. "Have you ever even been with a man besides him? Don't you want to know what it's like?"

"No!"

The shout surprised Aiden as much as Grímr and made the horse stumble. Aiden was shaking against the other man, considering pitching himself off the horse if this went on.

"I love him." Aiden's voice was raw with emotion, his eyes pleading for Grímr to understand, "What he's done, how he really feels, none of that matters. I love him, and that was my decision. You won't change that now."

Slowly, reluctantly, Grímr withdrew his hands.

"Fine," he said, with a tone of finality that Aiden couldn't read. But he didn't touch Aiden again.

They rode out of the valley as the sun began to sink in the sky, and as the golden afternoon waned toward a scarlet sunset, the two men spoke not a word to each other. Aiden's thoughts were far away, watching the painted clouds run down the horizon toward the blue gray sea visible from the mountainside they were climbing, as he thought about Grímr's words and wondered about Einarr's past. Where Grímr's thoughts were, Aiden couldn't see. The man's face was as unreadable as stone. So different from Einarr, whose feelings were always clear to Aiden, even when he did hide them behind that warm smile. Perhaps Einarr hid his feelings better from others, but he'd always been an open book to Aiden. Or at least, Aiden had always thought he was. Maybe he'd been overestimating his own abilities all this time. He couldn't shake his doubt and insecurity. He wished Einarr would hurry up and find them and banish all these pointless worries.

As the light was waning, Aiden began to wonder why Grímr hadn't stopped to make camp yet. It was better to choose a spot before darkness fell. But Grímr rode on in silence. And then, surprising Aiden so much he jumped, Grímr suddenly leaned closer over him again, his weight heavy on Aiden's back. Aiden started to protest and shove the other man away, until his fingers touched Grímr's skin and he realized how hot the other man was, his eyes glazed and unseeing with fever. Heart fluttering with panic, Aiden shook Grímr by the shoulders, trying to bring him back around. Instead, Grímr's eyes closed and he slumped against Aiden's back entirely, threatening to slide off the horse. Aiden caught him and the reins with a panicked yelp and steered the horse toward the closest friendly-looking tumble of rocks.

He only just managed to get the horse stopped before Grímr slid off, falling into the grass and not moving. Aiden struggled to get off the horse more gently, his broken leg howling in protest at the jarring motion. He threw the horse's reins over a rock and limped over to Grímr, rolling the man onto his back. His breathing was shallow and troubled, his skin burning hot to the touch. When Aiden pulled up his shirt, the redness of infection was visible even beyond the bandages he'd applied earlier. Too late, obviously. He unbound them, hoping that letting the wound air out might help. No wonder the man had been so unusually forward today. The fever must have already been affecting him.

He scrambled to build a fire before the light failed entirely, and then dragged Grímr into the dubious shelter of the stones, a few of which had fallen favorably enough to create a shallow cave. Aiden laid the other man out on a bed of moss and then found himself lost as for what to do next. What did you do to bring down a fever like this? How did you treat an infected wound? Aiden wished he'd paid more attention during the last battle to how their healer had dealt with these things. Maybe then, he could have helped Grímr somehow. Or at least not felt so completely useless.

"Please pull through this," Aiden begged the fever-addled man, dribbling water into his mouth. "I really don't want to starve to death out here alone."

Grímr didn't answer, only mumbling, lost in his fever dreams.

"Einarr," he said, over and over in his sickly sleep, "Einarr, Einarr."

Eventually, the fever broke and Grímr shook with chills. Aiden piled every bit of cloth or fur they had on him, but it seemed to make no difference. Aiden didn't know if this was better or worse than the fever— if this was improvement or further down spiral. Eventually, exhausted and out of ideas, he climbed under the piled blankets and curled up next to Grímr himself, hoping to warm him with his own heat if nothing else. So they passed the night, Aiden sleeping little for worry, waking often to check on Grímr, afraid every time that he would find the other man dead beside him. His thoughts were an anxious jumble, unsure if it would be better for the man to die while he risked waiting here for Einarr, or if he should be trying harder to save Grímr, for his own sake if nothing else. But what else he could be doing, Aiden didn't know. He'd rarely felt so powerless as he did now, laying with his arms around the man who'd stolen him, his head on Grímr's broad chest, listening to his rapid, fluttering heartbeat as he struggled to stay alive.

"What do I do?" he thought, begging any god that was listening, *"What else can I do? How do I save myself from this?"*

The next morning dawned damp and chilly, and Aiden crawled out from under the furs feeling worse than ever. His leg ached with every heartbeat, and his head swam. He wanted to curl up and ignore the world, but Grímr was in worse shape than him, and that meant he had no choice but to pull through this and try to keep his captor alive. He reached for the water skin, running low, to try and convince Grímr to drink, but as he turned around, the other man's arm shot out, grabbing Aiden by the wrist and making him drop the skin in surprise.

"How long was I asleep?" Grímr asked, his hands still burning like coals with fever.

"Only a night," Aiden reassured him. "Your wound is infected, and I don't know what to do about it."

"Yarrow," Grímr gasped, and at first, Aiden thought he was talking nonsense until he repeated the word, "Yarrow. Leaves like ferns, little white flowers with five petals, grows in bunches. Find it."

Aiden nodded at once, and Grímr collapsed back into the moss, exhausted by the effort of even that little speech. Aiden sat beside him, wondering how he was going to do what the man had asked. He could barely limp across the cave on his leg. He could never hope to go wandering over the mountain looking for flowers. But what else was he supposed to do? If

79

there was a chance this plant could save Grímr, how could he ignore it?

He limped outside, leaning on a pine branch he'd found while looking for firewood the night before. He looked at the horse appraisingly. It would be pain and risk getting on and off the thing, but it might better his chances if he didn't have to walk. He limped over to the horse, thanking the gods or Arnnjorn's brother-in-law that it was such a patient, placid beast, and also a short one, which was all that made it possible for Aiden to throw himself over its back in his condition. He dragged himself on, his leg burning with pain at even that brief strain. But he made it, and then he turned the horse toward the hills, his eyes peeled for white flowers, anxiety gnawing at his heart.

The morning was still new, the sky pale and clouded, promising rain. Wind swept the hillside, stirring the grass in ripples of green and gold, bright against the stark gray sky. Aiden saw a rabbit sprinting up the mountainside, brown as the earth and quick as the wind, and wished he had the strength to chase it or the knowledge to trap it. He hadn't eaten since the rabbit the night before last, and the hunger made him dizzy and numb and made focusing difficult. There were many flowers among the grass, and Aiden peered at them from the back of his horse, afraid if he got down from the horse for the wrong one he would never make it back on.

He didn't know how long he'd been searching before he stopped by a spring to refill the water skin. Sliding off the horse was more painful than he'd even anticipated, the landing sending shocks of pain through him that left him lying on the ground just trying to breathe for several minutes. When he could think clearly enough to move again, he dragged himself on his belly to the spring and dipped the water skin below the cool surface, glad that at least he could do this. He drank enough to satisfy himself as well, then looked up, noticing in the distance the valley they'd rode through the day before, a deep shadow driven between the feet of two rugged peaks. If he could get back on the horse, he thought, he could ride that way and maybe he would meet Einarr coming from the other direction. Or he might ride all the way back to Ingifast. He wouldn't starve before he got there, probably.

But that would mean leaving Grímr alone to die. It would serve him right, part of Aiden thought. The man had tried to kill him, had tried to kill Einarr. He wanted Aiden for nothing but a weapon against his enemy. But a traitorous part of Aiden remembered the gentleness of Grímr's hands in tending Aiden's wounds. The way he'd begged Aiden to love him, but pulled away when Aiden refused him. There was hardness, a cruelty there, absolutely. But there was kindness beneath it too, and a vast loneliness Aiden couldn't begin to understand. And there was the nervous, insecure part of Aiden that wanted Grímr alive if only to tell him what Einarr wouldn't. He could ride away now and take his chances. But he wouldn't. Beyond everything else, all the other fears and

81

desires, Aiden didn't have it in him to leave a man to die that way.

He turned back toward the horse, his decision made, and began dragging himself toward it, pausing when he heard a familiar buzzing near his ear. He shooed the bee away from him quickly, then felt his heart leap as he realized what that meant. He grabbed his pine branch and dragged himself to his feet, following the sound of further buzzing past the spring and into the small copse of scrubby trees, grinning widely when he saw a fat beehive hanging from a pine tree above a bed of white flowers. As he lit a small, smoky fire under the hive and began collecting flowers, he half expected a needle and thread to drop out of the hive as well. He made a note to leave an offering to Einarr's gods when he got home. This was too lucky to be anything but their work.

Chapter Eight

When he made it back to the cave, he woke Grímr, who groggily walked Aiden through the process of making a poultice with the yarrow and the honey. Aiden cleaned the wound again and spread the poultice in it, hoping it would be enough to help. Grímr stayed awake long enough to tell Aiden how to make a basic snare for rabbits before passing out again, and Aiden, though his leg sorely disagreed with the decision, limped back outside to set the traps. He couldn't place them very far from the camp, but he crossed his fingers and hoped that would be enough anyway. Then he fell into the moss beside Grímr, hoping sleep would ease the hunger pangs in his belly as well as the fierce, burning pain in his leg. He woke in the evening to check the snares, all but shaking with relief when he saw one had closed around a skinny hare.

He brought it home and cooked it, forcing Grímr to get up and eat a little before returning to his fever sleep. As night descended, rain fell, cold and misty just beyond the shallow cave, making the fire sputter and blowing into their poor shelter whenever there was a cross wind. Aiden's leg wouldn't hold his weight at all, but Aiden half walked, half crawled to fetch fallen pine boughs, still thick with needles, and drag them over the entrance of their shelter to shield his sleeping companion from the dampness. Then, he fell into the moss beside the other man and slept, dreaming of home. First of Einarr and Agna and Jódís, the warm comfort of the longhouse, lying among furs that smelled of the man he loved, the wooden beams of the house creaking in the winter wind, the soft breathing of his family around him, close by and safe. Then, he was back in England, lying between his mother and father, the sheep bleating outside, too young to be unhappy, just content to be among his family. And then it was years later when both of them were gone and it was just him in the same house, dusty and echoing with emptiness, so alone, he could feel it ache in his ribcage with every breath. He could stand on the vacant windswept moor while the spinning moon tumbled through its phases above like a whirling silver top and the stars hailed down around him in glittering liquid fire and scream at the blue black void all he liked, but God would not answer, and no one would be there when he returned to that dark and empty house, as he always would, too terrified of the unknown to try anything else. Until the falling stars caught the house on fire, and the faces of the villagers were pressed against the windows, screaming as everything around them burned...

And then he felt an arm around him, strong and warm, pulling him close. A voice murmured in his ear that everything was fine, that he was safe. He turned into that comfort and clung to it, shaking, imagining it with the face of Einarr or Arnnjorn or his father or his mother. Either way, his dreams settled and his shaking stopped and he fell back into dreamless darkness.

In the morning, he woke tangled around Grímr like a lover, curled up in his embrace the same way he usually slept with Einarr. Grímr's arms were wrapped around him, fingers tangled in his red hair. Blushing and baffled by the situation, Aiden carefully disentangled himself.

He limped out to check the traps first, which were empty, then came back and checked on Grímr's wound, cleaning out the poultice and replacing it. The skin around the wound looked less inflamed now. Aiden could only assume that was a good thing.

Grímr woke as Aiden finished bandaging the wound again, blinking up at Aiden tiredly.

"I'm glad you're awake," Aiden said more earnestly than he meant to. "You need to eat. I made broth from the rabbit last night. It isn't much, but it's better than nothing. I also tried making a tea out of the yarrow. I don't know if that will do anything, but I figured it was worth trying. I'm sorry that boiling things seems to be the extent of my abilities. Einarr didn't take me for my cooking skills."

Grímr chuckled at that, and Aiden helped the other man sit up before offering him the broth. Grímr sat quietly sipping his liquid meal for a while, examining the makeshift campsite Aiden had made them in the little cave.

"Thank you," he said after a time, "For caring for me. You've worked hard. You didn't have to."

"I would have died out here alone," Aiden replied with a shrug. "I wasn't going to make it home on a broken leg by myself."

85

"Somehow, I'm not certain that's true," Grímr replied, looking around them again at what Aiden had managed. "You're stronger than I thought you were."

Aiden, pleased but flustered by the compliment, looked away, busying himself with cleaning up something by the fire. Grímr continued to stare at him regardless.

"I can see why Einarr fought so hard for you."

Aiden paused, the words hitting him hard. He was tired and hungry and hurting, and all he wanted in the world was for Einarr to appear in the cave entrance and carry him home. But in the two nights they'd been here, Aiden had seen no sign of anyone following. It was entirely possible that Einarr assumed he was dead. It was not a thought Aiden wanted to entertain.

"Why did you stay?" Grímr asked, and Aiden looked back at him, eyes wary. "Why didn't you take the horse and ride for home when I was too weak to stop you?"

Aiden considered a variety of excuses, and finally settled on the one closest to the truth.

"I couldn't leave you to die alone," he replied, "Regardless of what you've done to me. I don't want to be the kind of person who could do that."

Grímr sat in silence, thinking about that for a long time while Aiden cleaned up the mess from breakfast.

"You should get some more rest," Aiden said eventually. "Your fever isn't gone yet."

"One more night," Grímr agreed, lying back down. "We can't afford to stay any longer than that."

The day passed slowly, the rain from the night before returning in fits and starts. Without much to do, Aiden talked to Grímr when the other man was awake, discussing only superficial things. How well Aiden's traps were doing, how miserable the weather was. It was easy, and it made it easy for Aiden to forget the animosity that had been between them so recently. When not discussing Einarr, Grímr was a quietly insightful person, slow to speak but with something meaningful to say when he did. And he was a good listener, quietly humoring Aiden's vigorous complaints about how the rabbits kept knocking over his snares without falling into them. Quite a change to the irritable brute constantly telling him to be quiet the day before. Aiden wasn't certain if it was the fever that had mellowed him, or something else.

In the evening, Grímr's fever returned, and Aiden watched him in heartsick worry as he writhed, senseless and burning. Aiden barely slept, eyes riveted to Grímr's pain-wracked features. In the morning, it had passed, but Grímr was so weak, he could barely move.

"One more night," he said, his voice shaking with exhaustion, "One more night."

One more night turned into two, then three, as Grímr fought off the infection eating him alive. Aiden cleaned and replaced the poultice, making regular trips to collect fresh water, more honey, check the snares, though every trip out seemed to make his leg

87

weaker and more pained. It never stopped hurting, but now the constant pain was a brand pressed against his bones rather than a pressed-bruise throb. Aiden was beginning to prefer the idea of starvation to the thought of having to get up and walk again.

"If you keep up like this," Grímr pointed out as Aiden returned from checking the snares and collapsed at once, shaking with pain and exhaustion, "You'll never walk on that leg again."

"Somebody has to keep us alive." Aiden's voice was shaky, though he tried for humor, "I don't see you getting up to catch us food, lazy bones."

"Ah, I admit it," Grímr chuckled, rubbing weakly at his tired eyes. "I've been faking all this time. It's just so entertaining watching you run around, waiting on me hand and foot."

Aiden laughed as well, though he didn't have much energy to put into it. He swallowed hard to stop the tears of pain and frustration that were trying to overwhelm him.

"It's been so long since anyone gave a damn about me," Grímr went on, his voice strained and oddly wistful. Aiden forced his eyes open to see Grímr staring at him with a kind of strange longing. Aiden's heart squeezed in his chest at the sight, and he looked away quickly, rejecting the well of feelings that tried to make themselves known.

"You still haven't told me what Einarr did, that's all," Aiden claimed, brusque as he rolled to face away from the other man.

"Well, that doesn't give me much incentive to tell you, does it," Grímr chuckled low again, and Aiden wasn't sure what the sinking feeling in his heart meant.

Chapter Nine

That night, Grímr woke again as Aiden was sitting in the cave entrance. It was a clear night for once, the stars bright and the moon massive, heavy and pendulous as it hung in the sky like a pregnant belly, full and round. But Aiden wasn't looking at the moon. He was looking down the mountain toward the valley, the place he was certain Einarr would come from, if Einarr came at all. The moon cast the sides of the peaks in silver and the valley itself in pitchest blue black shadow. The sharp contrast made it look like a painting, an illumination from one of the manuscripts Father Maredudd read from every Sunday in the village where he'd grown up. Stark and lovely, it was nonetheless not the sight Aiden wanted to see. Not so long as there was no spark in that shadowed valley of a campfire or a torch indicating someone was on their way through it.

"What are you doing up?" Grímr asked, voice thick with sleep. "You should rest."

Aiden didn't answer at first, thoughts preoccupied.

"Do you think he's dead?" he asked after a long moment, his chest tightening at the thought. "I know he would be coming after me if he could. So if he isn't, then something must be wrong, right?"

"He isn't dead," Grímr's expression was set with absolute certainty when Aiden looked back, highlighted silver by the moon. "I'd know if he was. I'd feel it. Einarr is definitely still alive."

Aiden looked away again, wondering if that was better or worse. He should be happy as long as Einarr was alive and well somewhere, but the thought that he'd been a passing interest to the other man, not worth coming after... There had to be another explanation. There were a dozen other reasons Aiden could think of that he wouldn't be here yet. But his thoughts dwelled only on the worst possibilities and wouldn't let him rest.

"He'll come for you," Grímr spoke again, though Aiden had assumed the other man had gone back to sleep. "I'm certain he will. If I'm wrong, then I'll just turn around and bring you back to him myself."

Aiden looked back at Grímr in confusion at this.

"There's not much point in my revenge if he doesn't care enough about you to chase," Grímr scoffed, lying down again, "But if I made you fall in love with me, that might get his attention."

Aiden, amused by the sentiment, smiled, but said nothing, returning his gaze to the night. Grímr was a strange man, made rough and unsociable by his long isolation. But there were the ruins of a good person under there somewhere. A certain gruff kindness lingered behind the bitter loneliness. Aiden wondered if, allowed to be around other people again, Grímr might still have a chance to become someone he could admire.

The next day, Grímr was feeling stronger, standing and moving on his own, for which Aiden was deeply relieved, finally able to rest his leg. In a reverse of how they'd lived the past few days, Grímr insisted Aiden stay lying in the furs while he went out to fetch water and check the snares. Aiden was happy to oblige, the very thought of putting weight on his leg making him feel like being sick. He watched the morning sun crawl across the ceiling of the cave, waiting for Grímr to return and wondering what would happen to them next. Would Grímr really turn around and go back if he decided Einarr wasn't following them? What would happen to Aiden if Einarr didn't want him anymore? The thought made his stomach knot with anxiety. He wouldn't be able to stay in Arnnstead without Einarr's protection, but he had nowhere else to go. As an English man with no master in this country, he might as well be an outlaw. He glanced toward the entrance of the little cave, thoughtful. If he asked to go with Grímr, would the outlaw accept him?

He sat up as he heard footsteps outside the cave, and a moment later Grímr hurried in, holding two rabbits, his face drawn.

"Get up," he said, gathering their things. "We need to get moving. We've lingered here too long."

Aiden, confused by the sudden urgency, nonetheless reached for his pine branch to try and pull himself up, biting back a whimper at the first motion of his leg.

"Never mind," Grímr appeared beside him, taking the stick out of his hand and pushing him back down, "Just sit there. Don't move."

Aiden obeyed, frowning as he watched Grímr tie the rabbits to the horse's saddle, shoving his things into his single, shabby bag with practiced haste. As soon as he was done, he scooped Aiden up so quickly that Aiden shouted in surprise, settling him on the horse before he climbed on after.

"Is something wrong?" Aiden asked, beginning to be worried by Grímr's obvious frantic haste. "Did you see something?"

"Everything's fine," Grímr lied obviously. "I'm just ready to get moving. We've wasted enough time."

Aiden didn't believe him, but he didn't argue either as Grímr nudged the horse, hurrying it away from their campsite and down the other side of the mountain slope. Positioned as he was in front of Grímr, Aiden couldn't look back to see if there was anything in the distance behind them, but a thin, nervous hope had sprouted in his chest and refused to be smothered.

Grímr pushed the horse harder than usual all day, stopping for nothing, until even Aiden could see the poor animal was reaching its limit.

"The sun is going down, anyway," he argued with Grímr. "If you try to keep riding in the dark, the horse will slip and break its leg, if it doesn't die of exhaustion first."

He was fairly exhausted himself, the constant motion of the horse meaning constant, painful jostling for his injured leg. He was pale and shivering in a cold sweat by now. Grímr looked down at him, jaw set like he was about to refuse anyway, but when he saw how weak Aiden looked, he finally slowed the horse at the top of a bare hill where they could see for a good distance around them in all directions.

"I need to check on your shoulder," Aiden said as Grímr lifted him off the horse, setting him down in the grass.

"I can tend it myself now," Grímr assured the smaller man, dragging the fur off the horse's back and throwing it over Aiden. "You should rest. Even I can tell you're struggling."

He was right, but Aiden didn't want to admit it. It had taken too much out of him tending the other man for so long. Aiden couldn't even stand on his own anymore. But still, as Grímr began starting a fire to cook the rabbits, Aiden turned his head to look down the hill back the way they had come. He almost thought he could see a light in the distance. His heart leapt, and he slept well that night.

Grímr woke him before sunrise, bundling him up in the fur without a word and putting him on the horse. Confused and half-awake, Aiden looked back before his view was obscured by Grímr swinging onto the horse behind him, and saw a trail of smoke in the distance from a fire.

"It's him," he said out loud, and Grímr's arms tightened around him as he urged the horse forward faster.

They didn't speak all day, Grímr responding to all Aiden's attempts with wordless grunts. Aiden's heart hardly seemed to slow once seeing that smoke on the horizon started it hammering. Einarr was alive and coming for him. This would all be over soon.

Once again, he had to beg Grímr to let the horse rest when evening came.

"Damn the horse, then," Grímr snarled as he pulled it to a stop, swinging down and lifting Aiden off. "We'll walk!"

"He'll only catch you faster," Aiden argued. "You know he's on a horse as well. And besides, if you push yourself too much, your fever will come back and you won't be able to run at all."

"Are you on my side or his?" Grímr snapped, irritated, and Aiden realized quite suddenly that he wasn't sure.

He lay awake until the other man's breathing evened out with sleep, then sat up, looking back the way they had come. He could see the light clearly now, closer than it had been before. But Grímr's words still troubled him. Whose side was he on? He wanted to see Einarr again. He wanted to know the truth. But he didn't want Grímr to be hurt, either. And if Grímr and Einarr met now, Aiden was certain it would be a fight to the death. The obvious answer then, Aiden realized, was to leave now. He would go back to Einarr, and Grímr would be able to escape. He shifted his leg and bit his lip to stifle a pained noise. He couldn't get there by walking. He'd have to take the horse. He had managed to pull himself onto it before; he could do it again.

He moved slowly, carefully sliding out of the furs without waking Grímr, and then he dragged himself toward the horse as quietly as he could, his leg already throbbing. It wouldn't hurt much longer, he told himself. Back in Arnnstead with Einarr, he could see the healer and have it properly treated and rest until it was healed again. He just needed to go a little further first.

The horse was still bridled, but not saddled, but if Aiden could get himself across its back and point it in the right direction, that would be enough. He could hold on from there.

He pulled himself up, using the horse for support, a soft gasp of pain escaping him as soon as his leg touched the ground. Still, he tensed himself to jump, ready to throw himself over its back. He sprang, then slid. He hadn't jumped far enough. He landed hard on his bad leg and cried out in pain, unable to prevent the noise. The horse whinnied in surprise at the shout so close to it and the yank on its reins, which Aiden grabbed as he slid. It reared and bolted, and Aiden, his hand caught in the reign, was dragged with it. He shouted in fear, no longer worried about being stealthy, struggling to disentangle his wrist as the horse fled in the wrong direction. He bounced through the rocky dirt, barely able to see to disentangle the knot, certain he was about to be dragged to his death, when a large hand suddenly caught the reins, and then him, yanking the horse back and pulling Aiden clear of its flailing hooves. Aiden, paralyzed with fear, clung to the other man's chest as Grímr fought to calm the panicked horse.

"What the hell were you doing?" Grímr demanded as soon as he had the horse tied up. "You could have killed yourself!"

"I was trying to help!" Aiden shouted back, adrenaline still rushing from his near trampling. "Einarr is gaining on us, and if he catches you, he'll kill you!"

"Idiot! I want him to catch us!" Grímr insisted, putting Aiden down gently in the grass despite his anger. "Haven't you been listening all this time? Do you not understand that I want to fight him?"

"Then why have you been running like the Devil was at your heels for the past two days?" Aiden pointed out, his eyes flashing, "When you were so at peace before, thinking he wouldn't follow? I don't believe for a second that you intend to spend the rest of your life leaving parts of me at his door. You went to him wanting to die, but then you changed your mind. Why?"

"Why do you care?" Grímr bellowed back, leaning over Aiden. "Why do you care how I choose to die?"

"Because I want you to live, of course!"

Grímr recoiled, stunned by Aiden's frank confession.

"Just let me go back to him," Aiden demanded. "Put me on the horse and point me in the right direction. Then go out of the country and find somewhere to start again. I won't let him come after you. So go and live!"

Grímr, for a moment, looked so lost that Aiden's heart ached, wishing there was any other way to repair this situation. He wanted to reach out to Grímr, to hold on to him and keep him steady. It wasn't love, at least not like what he felt for Einarr, but he desperately wanted to save Grímr.

Then the outlaw's expression changed, hardening into unreadable stone.

"No," he said, his voice a low growl as he leaned down to speak directly to Aiden's face, "You seem to have forgotten that you're my prisoner. You don't get a say in what I do with you. And I am *never* letting him have you."

Aiden's heart raced, realizing the mistake he'd made. Grímr didn't want saving. This was a man who'd done nothing but survive for years, because he could only stand to be destroyed by one man. It would not be so easy to convince him to live.

"Don't you realize what will happen if he finds you?" Aiden pleaded, catching Grímr's shirt to keep him close. "You won't win with that wound! I'll have to watch him kill you. I don't want that!"

For a moment, a kind of desperate hope flickered in Grímr's eyes, then quickly died. He threw Aiden's hand off and moved away.

"Do you think I would give up my revenge just for you?" he shouted, pain in his eyes despite his anger. "What do you think you are to me?"

"I—" Aiden wasn't sure how to answer. He suspected Grímr's feelings for him were deep, but...

"All you are to me is a way to hurt him!"

Aiden's eyes widened, the words cutting like a knife. He stared at Grímr, pain and disbelief plain in his eyes. But Grímr said nothing more, only turned away, hurrying to get them ready to go.

Grímr saddled the still nervous horse and put Aiden on it, moving quickly though it was still too dark to ride safely. Grímr rode anyway, glancing behind them anxiously and often, as the light in the distance grew ever closer. Aiden rode stiffly in front of him, head spinning as he searched for the right words, the right actions, to see this end without Einarr or Grímr dead.

Dawn greyed the sky behind them while Grímr raced to keep up with the fleeing night. The sun spilled over the jagged horizon and lit up the figure of a lone man on a horse, riding after them, too far away for any feature to be distinct. Still, Aiden knew with perfect certainty that it was Einarr, and that they would not outrun him for long. Still, he didn't have the courage to say another word to Grímr, still wounded against all sense by the other man's words. He didn't know why he'd thought their relationship was anything more than captor and captive, but at some point in the cave, or maybe even before that, his pity had overwhelmed his fear of the other man, and he'd forgotten his situation, deluding himself with dreams where everyone came out of this unscathed and happy.

Grímr's breath was ragged in his ear. The man had been pushing himself too hard so soon after his illness. He was going to collapse again if he kept up

99

this way— Aiden could see it. He wanted to beg Grímr to stop, but he didn't know what to say that he hadn't already said. It seemed too dire a situation to correct.

He looked ahead as the sun began to lighten the sky ahead of them, frowning as he saw lines of smoke running across the pale dawn colors. They surprised Grímr too, who pulled the horse up short to stare.

"Is there a town here?" Aiden asked, forgetting the tension for a moment in confusion. He would have thought an outlaw like Grímr would be experienced at avoiding villages and settlements.

"Be quiet," Grímr replied, forgetting nothing. Aiden obeyed as Grímr cautiously urged his horse forward again. As they crested the hill, it became clear the smoke was not from a town, but from dozens of fires, scattered across the encampment of a vast resting army. Aiden stared, staggered by the sheer number of tents and men moving among them. He'd only seen so many men together once before. As he glimpsed the pointed banners waving over the encampment, emblazoned with the image of a rearing bear, he realized they were the same group of men. This was the army of Jarl Bjorn, who'd only this winter attempted to take Arnnstead. But why were they gathered? Aiden thought the Jarl didn't intend to gather his forces until summer to go raiding. Had those rumors been a ploy, keeping the coastal village's guards down while he prepared? Aiden knew he intended to unify all of the northern clans. Could he be beginning war again now, before the planting was

100

even finished? Aiden wondered if Bjorn's promise to leave Arnnstead in peace would hold true.

Grímr glanced back at the hills behind them again warily, but the silhouette of the following figure wasn't visible, lost among the many peaks and shadowed places.

"We'll have to go through them," he said, nodding decisively.

"What?" Aiden stared at the other man in utter bafflement. "You can't be serious. Do you see how many there are?"

"They lay between us and the sea," Grímr pointed out. "I have a boat prepared on that coast to take us out of here. It will take us an extra day to go around them, and in the meantime, that brute behind us will catch up."

"So, you'd rather be killed by Jarl Bjorn instead?" Aiden said in a sarcastic hiss. "If they guess you're an outlaw, any of those warriors would be glad to claim the honor of putting you down."

"I have no intention of being killed," Grímr said, staring back the way he'd come coldly. "We will go at night. We won't be seen. And hopefully, the sight of this army will slow our pursuer."

"You're mad," Aiden declared. "The fever burned out your brain."

"Well, this madman owns you right now." Grímr turned the horse away from the army, scanning the area nearby for a good place to camp until nightfall. "So you had better hope I'm not too mad to pull this off."

They huddled among the rocks, watching the comings and goings of the army as they waited for nightfall. Grímr kept a more wary eye on the horizon they'd come from than the one they were headed for. Aiden could feel his tension at the time they were losing as Einarr closed the gap between them. Judging by how far back he'd been the last time Aiden had seen him, if he rode without stopping, he'd be on them by tonight. Aiden was no longer sure if he wanted Einarr to catch up to them. If he did, it was certain to be a deadly confrontation. Hurt as he was by Grímr shutting him out, he still didn't want the other man killed. There had to be some way to fix this situation, even if Aiden couldn't figure out what it was yet.

The long day passed in tense silence. Aiden gave up for now on trying to talk sense into Grímr, watching the army instead. He saw no sign of Jarl Bjorn, though he saw plenty of the Jarl's son, Hallvaror. A mighty and renowned warrior with golden hair, Hallvaror was the type of man born to have saga written about him, and he knew it. Aiden had only met him briefly, but the man was dangerously ambitious, cleverness and strength untempered by wisdom or caution. Aiden was just glad the young warrior still had his father to keep him in check until he was a little older and more thoughtful. Bjorn was ambitious too, but not to the point of self-destruction.

Later in the day, just as even Aiden was beginning to get restless, a smaller force arrived to join the larger army, coming from the coast. Aiden couldn't believe they needed even more men. It seemed preposterous that they needed as many as they already had. But the newcomers set up tents and settled in, their leader heading to a central tent where, presumably, Jarl Bjorn was waiting to meet them.

Dusk arrived, painting the sky in vibrant scarlet and orange that faded into lavender and then deep red purple. The men in the encampment below gathered to drink and boast and make merry, which worried Aiden. They'd sleep harder if they were drunk, but they'd also stay up later, increasing the chances that Einarr would find them before it was safe to cross through the camp. Though, if Aiden were truthful, it would never be safe to sneak through such a force.

But as the night grew deeper, blue black replacing the scarlet sunset with dazzling stars, Einarr did not appear. Perhaps he'd stopped, or lost track of them. Aiden imagined the other man standing in the cave where he and Grímr had sheltered, looking at the abandoned bandages, the marks of their brief life there, and wondering what had become of the two of them. Aiden wanted to see him again so much, it ached. His fickle heart swung back and forth between the desperate desire to be reunited with his lover, and the fear that such a reunion was bound to be spoiled by a lethal confrontation between Einarr and Grímr.

At last, the fires in the camp began to go out, and Aiden and Grímr both watched as the men, drunk and happy, stumbled off to their tents to sleep. Soon, the camp looked nearly empty, only a few drunkards still awake, drinking too long and bound to regret it in the morning.

"It's time," Grímr said.

He placed Aiden on the back of the horse, pulling a cloak up over his head, then took the horse's reins and, walking beside it, led it down into the camp. There were no sentries. This army didn't believe it had any enemies to watch out for at the moment. But caution was still necessary. Norsemen at war slept lightly, often sitting up and always with weapons close at hand, ready to spring up at the slightest hint of danger. If they caused even the slightest disturbance, they would have the entire camp awake and on them in minutes. So they moved with great slowness and caution, taking their time as they passed through the center of the encampment. The sounds of men snoring, heavy with drink, surrounded them on all sides. The whicker and smell of horses was everywhere, the ground churned up to mud by hooves and boots. Aiden flinched at every creak of a tent in the breeze, certain at any moment that disaster would fall. If he got out of this alive, he made a mental note to kiss Arnnjorn's brother-in-law for raising such hardy and well-behaved horses. Small or not, Aiden had never met such a patient animal, to have been treated so roughly these past few days and still be so mild and manageable.

The two men froze as they heard drunken voices approaching, and Grímr quickly pulled the horse out of sight behind a large tent. They watched as two warriors, both of them stumbling drunk, wandered into view, laughing to each other about some mischief, their words too slurred to understand. Their arms around each other, they tottered blindly toward Aiden's hiding place. He saw Grímr's hand move slowly toward Arnnjorn's sword hanging at his waist, and Aiden tensed with fear, anticipating a confrontation.

"You two! What are you doing there?"

Aiden jumped as someone stepped around a nearby tent, shouting at the two drunkards. As the man stepped into the light of the moon, Aiden realized it was Hallvaror.

"Get to your tents, both of you," he snapped at the drunk warriors, "If you're too ill to march in the morning, I'll have you both whipped like dogs."

One of the men attempted a blustering, belligerent reply, but his friend grabbed him and dragged him off with an apology, hurrying toward their tents and away from where Aiden and Grímr were hiding. Aiden watched as Hallvaror turned toward the tent they were hiding behind, stepping inside it.

"Son," a familiar voice spoke from within the tent, catching Aiden's attention, "What are you still doing wandering at this hour?"

It was Jarl Bjorn's voice, and realizing that made Aiden stiffen with surprise. He leaned closer, peering toward a gap in the folds where candle light showed through.

Bjorn, a tall, thin-faced man with a sour temperament, stood at a roughly constructed table looking over maps. His son, handsome and gallant-looking as ever, stood near the mouth of the tent.

"I could ask you the same," Hallvaror replied and, though Aiden couldn't really see his face through the tent, he assumed the younger man was smiling. "You should rest. Now that Torvaldr and his men have joined us, we may march in the morning."

Still bent over his maps, Bjorn shook his head.

"No, no, there's still two other clans at least sending men, and all the others rushed their planting for our sake. It was only for you I began gathering them this soon. You must have more patience, my son."

"We have enough men without the other clans," Hallvaror said with a huff. "Enough to ravage Vinland all summer. Or to do much more here. The coastal villages have begun fighting amongst themselves again already."

Grímr tried to lead the horse on, but Aiden waved a hand to stop him, wondering if he might risk calling out to the Jarl. Bjorn was close with Arnnjorn. He might return Aiden if he asked for help. But would he also spare Grímr at Aiden's request?

Bjorn sighed wearily.

"We have talked about this, Hallvaror." Bjorn sounded tired and Aiden imagined the man rubbing his temples, though he couldn't see it. "I will conquer no more in the north. It was a mistake to claim so much in the first place."

"It wasn't a mistake," Hallvaror insisted. "Your only mistake is in stopping now. The English grow

106

bolder every day, destroying our settlements on the Northumbrian coast. We need to be unified to defeat them!"

"Don't you see that's why I had to stop?" Bjorn replied as Grímr tried to pull the horse on and Aiden once again waved him away. "I was so fixated on defending us against the English, I nearly destroyed us myself. Destroyed what makes us who we are. With every village I forced to my way of doing things, so much was lost. Stories and songs and traditions going back generations. The English will never conquer us with swords, but every day, they take a little more of us, anyway. Our people abandon the old ways for English novelties. Christian missionaries turn them from their fathers' gods. And I have helped them, made it easier for them, by loosening those ties. It is more important for us to retain our heritage than to expand."

"There won't be any heritage to protect if we let the English defeat us!" Hallvaror sounded frustrated, and Aiden saw him moving closer to his father. "But you won't change your mind, will you? You've become soft in your old age. A coward who flees the battle on the verge of victory."

Aiden's eyes widened, stunned by the tremendous insult. He'd lived with the Northmen long enough to know that to call someone a coward that way was to all but ask them to kill you, and that it would be fully within the law for them to do so.

"How dare you−" Bjorn began to say, rising from his table. He didn't finish the statement. Aiden jumped as he saw Hallvaror suddenly dart closer to his father, the brief shine of a blade reflecting in the lamplight. Then there was only the sound of labored, gurgling breaths.

"I won't let you doom our people," Hallvaror hissed, "Nor will I waste all you've built. Don't worry, Father. I will make certain no one ever forgets your name."

Aiden, horrified, tore his eyes away to stare at Grímr, who stared back in equal shock. They heard movement in the tent— Hallvaror shifting the body— and Grímr quickly pulled on the horse's reins again. Aiden let him, shivering with the magnitude of what he'd just seen. Hallvaror had murdered his father and intended to steal his army to attack the coast. Aiden was too stunned to even think straight. By the time he could gather his thoughts again, they had reached the other side of the camp at last.

"We have to go back," Aiden said once they were clear of the tents, reaching down to grab Grímr's shoulder.

"Go back?" Grímr repeated, flabbergasted, "We just got out!"

"We have to warn Arnnstead and the other coastal towns!" Aiden explained, hands trembling. "They won't stand a chance against that army if he takes them by surprise."

"And why exactly should I give a damn?" Grímr argued. "We're leaving. It's of no concern to us."

"It's of concern to me!" Aiden argued. "There are people I care about in that town!"

"Einarr can take care of himself—"

"I'm not talking about Einarr!" Aiden shouted, and Grímr reached up to block his mouth, hushing him and looking back toward the camp nervously. Aiden pulled the other man's hand away and continued anyway. "Do you honestly think he's the only person in my life? I have friends in Arnnstead! Family! I won't leave them to be slaughtered because of this feud!"

"Well, I'm not going back." Grímr's eyes flashed threateningly, gripping Aiden's arm hard enough to hurt. "And, in case you've forgotten, I'm the one in charge, here."

"Then I'll go by myself!" Aiden kicked hard at Grímr's head with his good leg, hoping to catch the other man by surprise, only for Grímr to duck the blow and grab him by the thigh. Aiden struggled, swinging a fist at him and trying to throw himself off the horse. In response, Grímr only dragged him closer, his face pressed against Aiden's stomach while Aiden, half on the horse, half in Grímr's arms, struggled to get loose, boxing Grímr's ears.

"You'll die, you idiot!" Grímr shook him, trying to get Aiden to come to his senses, his breath hot against Aiden's belly. "I won't let you kill yourself!"

"You wanted to kill me to begin with!" Aiden squirmed and twisted, and Grímr pulled him away from the horse. "Your revenge is spoiled already, so just let me go!"

"No!" Grímr turned and fell, holding Aiden to him until he could press the smaller man into the grass. Aiden cried out as his injured leg hit the ground and he stopped fighting, shaking as the pain briefly overwhelmed him. Grímr lay between his legs, head still against Aiden's stomach, arms around Aiden's thighs. They lay there breathless for a moment, Aiden flustered by the compromising position, Grímr staring at him intently.

"I want you alive," Grímr demanded, squeezing Aiden's legs. "I want you with me."

"Why?" Aiden demanded as Grímr shifted, moving over him. "Why bother? And don't say it's revenge— I don't believe it! I want the truth!"

In response, Grímr's mouth collided with Aiden's, rough and passionate. His tongue forced its way past Aiden's lips, his hands squeezing Aiden's hips, pulling him closer. Heat rushed through Aiden, an immediate and undeniable reaction leaving his skin tingling in its wake. Aiden's hands clutched the front of Grímr's shirt, trying to push him away, and at last, Grímr released him, moving back only an inch. Speechless, Aiden could only stare up at him, wide-eyed, breathless, and red-faced with embarrassment. Grímr, as though he thought his point had been missed, leaned in to try and kiss Aiden again. Aiden put his hands up to block the other man at once.

"No!" he said reflexively, though his body was still flushed with warmth from the first kiss. His heart was fluttering like a trapped bird, his body at odds with his mind, which thought only of Einarr. He stared at Grímr warily, half afraid the other man would continue in spite of his refusal, some dark part of him hoping he would. He'd been ignoring his growing

110

attraction to the other man, pushing it off as just attachment because of their shared dependency. But it had grown even without his approval, and he knew Grímr could tell he wasn't rejecting the kiss out of hate.

"Why do you love him?" Grímr begged instead, not forcing any more on Aiden, though his eyes were broken with desperation. "Why are you so loyal to him? Am I so terrible that you would die just to get away from me?"

"This isn't about him or you," Aiden answered, summoning his resolve despite how anxious and unsure he felt. "I can't let all those people die when I could do something. Come with me or don't, but I won't go any further with you."

Grímr looked away, his expression strained, but then he moved away, taking Aiden's hand. Aiden sat up slowly, wondering if he'd finally gotten through to the other man. A second later, he realized his mistake as Grímr, pulling a rope from his bag, bound Aiden's hands. Aiden struggled to pull his hands away, crying out in protest, but Grímr only tightened the bonds and lifted Aiden like a sack of grain, throwing him over the back of the horse. Grímr swung up behind Aiden, ignoring the younger man's protests and pleas, and rode away from the encampment toward the sea.

The coast was not far from the encampment— less than a day's ride— and Grímr rode through the night despite the danger to the horse. Aiden complained and begged and cried until he was exhausted, but Grímr replied only with stoic silence, refusing to acknowledge any of it. Finally, too tired to continue trying to shout down a mountain, Aiden hung silently in his uncomfortable position, realizing he'd misjudged Grímr's capacity for cruelty.   Arnnstead, his family, all those people— they were going to die, and he couldn't do anything about it. He wouldn't even be here to try. His heart was at war with itself, crying pity for Grímr, desperate to help the broken man somehow, hungry for the way the other man looked at him sometimes like Aiden was the only thing keeping him breathing. The other half of him said Aiden should have aimed better with his axe. If he could just get back to Einarr, he knew all this confusion would end. If he could just see Einarr again, ask him the truth...

Chapter Ten

He woke to the sound of the ocean, a gentle roar in his ears. Grímr slid off the horse and lifted Aiden off with him, setting the younger man in the grass as he went down to the beach to drag a small boat out from where it was hidden among the rocks. He checked it over and got it ready before coming back and beginning to unsaddle the horse.

"Coward."

Grímr's hands stilled on the straps of the saddle for a moment as Aiden spoke, his voice calm but intense against the rush of the vast black sea that rolled against the white beach beside them.

"I was an idiot to think an outlaw could have any sense of honor," Aiden went on, refusing to let his voice shake despite the torrent of emotions within him which would have put those white-capped waves to shame. "An army is coming to destroy the lives of hundreds of your countrymen, and you are running away."

Grímr began silently working on the saddle again, not turning to look even as Aiden's voice rose with outrage, tears stinging his eyes.

"The same way you ran from Einarr when you saw him pursuing us!" Aiden spat like venom. "You're a coward, and I can't believe I wanted to help you!"

Still, Grímr didn't turn, so, tears running down his cheeks, Aiden reached for the only weapon he had.

"I may have been a thrall. I may yet be an argr. But it's you who was never a man. I despise you."

It was a lie— Aiden felt it in his heart— but he said it anyway, and he saw Grímr grow still, his back to Aiden but his shoulders tense with an emotion Aiden couldn't guess. Anger? Shame? Guilt? He leaned forward, resting his head against the horse's shoulder. The horse whickered, and looked back to nose him curiously. Aiden waited, his heart pounding, for the consequences. Slowly, Grímr's hands let go of the straps of the saddle.

"You don't hate me," he said with quiet certainty.

Aiden said nothing. Grímr turned, and Aiden caught his breath at the pain he saw in the outlaw's eyes. Grímr knelt in front of him, those endless, pleading eyes darker than the sea.

"Please, say you don't hate me," Grímr begged without a hint of shame. "You can't ask me to live with myself if you're telling the truth. Please."

Aiden only stared back at him in silence. It might not be true now, but if Grímr left those people to die, Aiden knew it would be. Grímr hung his head, giving up.

"You realize you've doomed me with this," he said, reaching out to untie Aiden's hands. "If you make me go back, either Einarr will kill me, or his uncle will demand my death."

"I won't let it happen," Aiden promised, relief overwhelming him. "Whatever else happens, I won't let it end that way."

Grímr looked like he doubted it, but with Aiden untied, he turned away and went to build a fire.

114

"We won't get back around that encampment tonight," he said. "In the morning, we'll take this boat around the coast. It'll be slower than going over land, but we should still be faster than a force of men that large, and we won't have to run the risk of meeting their scouts on the way."

"And you won't change your mind halfway there and take us out to sea, will you?" Aiden asked, a little suspicious.

"I told you," Grímr sighed as he gathered driftwood, "I can't stand you thinking of me as a coward. I was looking for a way to die, anyway. Perhaps if I die doing something so stupidly noble, I'll make it to the halls of Asgard, after all."

"If they won't take you," Aiden said with a smile, "They certainly won't take me. So, you can follow me to whatever afterlife is chosen for heretic argr thralls."

"It's a deal." Grímr laughed bitterly, and Aiden sat close to him once the fire was built, their arms touching as they shared the warmth against the cold night.

"You never did tell me what Einarr did," Aiden mused as, wrapped in a single fur, they waited for sleep or sunrise. "What happened to make you an outlaw?"

"I meant to save it," Grímr murmured. "To convince you to turn your back on Einarr. But I couldn't say the words. I've held on to my hate for him for so long..."

"Whatever it is," Aiden said, shaking his head, "I doubt it could make me hate him. I want to learn more about him because I love him. If something that happened so long ago could change my feelings for him, then maybe my feelings for him were never true to begin with."

Grímr eyed Aiden thoughtfully.

"If it did change your feelings for him," Grímr asked, "Could you learn to love me instead?"

Aiden fixed Grímr with a solemn, disapproving stare. Grímr shrugged and looked away.

"Then perhaps it's better I don't tell you. Perhaps you should hear it from him."

Aiden didn't push any farther, and for a few hours, they dozed, Aiden leaning on Grímr's shoulder as the night paled into a thin and watery dawn.

Chapter Eleven

Aiden woke as Grímr was suddenly yanked away from him, the sudden jerk shocking him into immediate, adrenaline-fueled wakefulness as the stranger threw Grímr to the ground and pointed a sword at his throat.

"Einarr!" Aiden cried, half cry of surprised delight, half warning.

The tall blond man looked angrier than Aiden had ever seen him, his handsome face a mask of rage, half covered in a strip of dark cloth that hid his left eye. Grímr, his weapon out of reach, could only stare up at Einarr as the other man advanced on him, sword raised, clearly ready to kill him.

And yet, Einarr hesitated. His jaw was clenched in anger, his hands white-knuckled on the hilt of his sword, and yet he couldn't bring it down. Aiden watched, horrified and helpless, expecting to see Grímr die, but Einarr only stood, shaking with anger and doing nothing.

Grímr, seeing his chance, flung a fistful of sand into Einarr's face. Einarr recoiled, and Grímr darted for his sword, raising it to defend himself just in time to block Einarr's wild swing, still blinded by the sand. Grímr took the advantage, lunging after Einarr, who struggled to defend himself, squinting sand out of his one good eye.

"Please, stop!" Aiden begged, trapped where he was by his leg and paralyzed by fear. "Don't hurt him!"

He wasn't sure which of the men he was shouting at. Either, both. He just wanted this to end.

And it did, as Grímr dove past Einarr's defenses to plant a shoulder in the other man's chest, driving him to the ground. The outlaw knelt above Einarr, sword pointed at Einarr's throat... and again, stopped.

The two men stared at each other, their eyes locked and full of rage, but neither moved, neither took the killing blow. Grímr's hands shook around his weapon. He shouted in frustration.

"Twenty years!" he howled. "Twenty years alone, planning revenge, and now you're here and I— Why? Why can't I do it?"

He thrust his sword into the sand beside Einarr's head and threw himself back, holding his head in tortured frustration. Einarr slowly sat up, catching his breath, and then miserably threw his sword to the side. Neither one of them could kill the other.

"I'm sorry," Einarr said, voice heavy with guilt and misery, all the anger drained away. "I didn't—"

"You abandoned me!" Grímr snapped, still plenty angry for both of them, "You left me to die, for your crimes!"

"It wasn't like that," Einarr protested. "I was a kid; I was scared—"

"Did you think I wasn't?" Grímr laughed cruelly. "I was terrified, and you let me face that alone. I would never have done that to you!"

"How do you know?" Einarr shouted back, getting angry again. "How do you know what you would have done? You murdered a woman in cold blood just to get to me! You kidnapped and tortured an innocent man— I should kill you! If I could kill you—"

"Einarr!" Aiden interrupted them, confused and afraid, and at last, the two men stopped shouting. Grímr still lay on the sand as Einarr crawled over to Aiden, pulling him close.

"I've been so afraid." Einarr's voice was rough with emotion, and Aiden could feel the other man shaking. "Are you hurt? Did he touch you?"

"I'm fine, mostly," Aiden reassured Einarr, closing his eyes for a moment to just bask in the warmth of Einarr's chest beneath his cheek, wreathed in the familiar scent of him. "I hurt my leg trying to get away, but other than that, I'm fine."

Aiden shook his head then, pushing away to look Einarr in the eye.

"There's more important things to think about right now," he said. "You saw Jarl Bjorn's army?"

"I did," Einarr confirmed, frowning.

"It's not Jarl Bjorn's anymore," Aiden explained. "We saw Hallvaror murder his father. He intends to lead that army against the coastal villages. Grímr was taking me back to warn everyone."

Einarr's frown deepened, and he looked past Aiden to Grímr, who was by then slowly getting to his feet. Einarr squeezed Aiden closer reflexively, and then moved to stand in front of the younger man.

"I'm surprised to learn he has that much honor left." Einarr glared at Grímr, ready to attack him at the slightest provocation. "An outlaw who would rather murder an innocent woman to lure me into a trap rather than challenge me like a man."

"I didn't kill that woman," Grímr replied, unable to look at Einarr or Aiden as he shook the sand from his pants, looking hollow and lost. "The men of Ingifast killed her. I only saw it happen and decided to use it to my advantage. It seems like Ingifast is just a breeding ground for murderers, isn't it?"

To Aiden's surprise, Einarr suddenly glanced toward him, guilt in his eyes. When he saw only confusion in Aiden's expression, he glared at Grímr again.

"No, I haven't told him," Grímr confirmed, bending to pick up his sword. "I thought I'd let you tell him yourself. I was honestly surprised he didn't know. When I found out you hadn't told him, I started to doubt you'd care enough to come after him at all."

Aiden, frightened the fighting was about to start again, darted around Einarr to grab Grímr's sword himself, forgetting his leg. He fell with a pained shout, but he got his hands on the sword, gripping it tightly even as he sprawled on the ground with his leg screaming fire at him. He saw Grímr moving toward him, and for a moment he was afraid the outlaw would try to wrestle it from him, but Grímr knelt by his leg instead.

"Idiot!" Grímr snapped, straightening Aiden's leg. "Did you forget you were hurt? I keep telling you not to move—"

"Get your hands off of him."

Einarr's voice was cold as ice, cold as the iron blade pressed to Grímr's neck. Grímr froze, his hands still on Aiden's leg. Aiden reached out instead to push that sword away.

"Stop, Einarr!" he said, still pale and shaky from the pain. "He was trying to help me. You don't need to hurt him."

"What has he done to you?" Einarr asked, eyes narrowed in suspicion, "What has he done to make you defend him like this?"

"He hasn't done anything—" Aiden tried to protest, but Grímr cut him off.

"Nothing you didn't do to him first," Grímr said, low and mocking. "How did you get him on your side after you put your collar on him?"

Einarr's face went red, but before he could react, Aiden had already slapped Grímr hard across the cheek.

"Stop it!" Aiden shouted. "I thought you wanted to fight him as equals! Have you changed your mind? Do you want him to cut you down like a coward now?"

Grímr clenched his jaw and looked away, anger and desperation in his eyes. Aiden knew Grímr himself wasn't sure of his plan anymore. He'd swung back and forth between wanting his revenge and just wanting to die since Aiden had met him. Now that he had realized he didn't have it in him to kill Einarr, he seemed set on goading the other man into killing him. He didn't really know what he wanted, that much was obvious.

Aiden looked up at Einarr, hoping the other man would take the hint and back off.

"Whatever happened between you," Aiden said, looking at Einarr with pleading eyes, "It can wait. We have to warn Arnnstead about Hallvaror's army. That's more important than any of us."

Einarr hummed reluctantly and lowered his sword, still looking at Grímr with mistrust in his eyes.

"He tried to kill you, Aiden," Einarr pointed out. "Snatched you away right in front of my eyes. For days, I thought I'd find what was left of you over every hill. I can't forgive him for that. I don't know how you can."

"Well that makes two of us, then," Grímr added without looking at either of them. "I have no intention of forgiving you, either."

Aiden held his breath, a distress he hadn't expected coursing through him as he looked between the two men.

"I would never ask you to forgive me for that," Einarr said with surprising softness. "I'm not proud of it. I deserve your hate. But you should never have brought Aiden into this."

Grímr's expression softened for a moment, and Aiden could see the aching desperation in the other man's eyes for some kind of resolution, be it death or anything else. Whatever was between them was torturing Grímr.

"Then just let him go," Aiden offered, looking up at Einarr. "Now that you're here, you can take me back to warn the others. And Grímr can just leave."

He looked at the other man, hoping Grímr would accept.

"You can just go," he pleaded. "Get out of this country. Start again."

There was a moment of silence on that still beach, the waves rolling ceaselessly behind them, as Einarr considered the offer and Grímr, stubbornly, remained where he was.

"I won't kill you," Einarr said finally. "I can't. I can't bring you back to be killed, either. Whatever you think of me— and I deserve whatever you think of me— I could never do that. So leave. Take the horse and go. Find somewhere to be happy."

Grímr seemed to wilt, closing his eyes, his lips drawing back over his teeth in an expression of despair that left Aiden speechless.

"Please, Grímr," Aiden said gently. "This is the best way. I don't want to see either of you hurt."

Grímr's jaw was tense, and Aiden's words only seemed to make it tighter. But at last, he let go of Aiden's hand and stood slowly, keeping his eyes on Einarr.

"His leg is broken." Grímr headed for his horse, showing no signs of fighting. "And he's walked on it too much, despite my efforts. He needs to stay off it completely. If you take the boat, watch out for the currents around the cape."

The point of Einarr's sword dropped into the sand, and he watched Grímr go with an expression of hollow devastation. Aiden watched him go, confused by the way his heart twisted to see the outlaw leaving.

"Hey," he called after Grímr, worried, "Be careful, okay? That wound on your shoulder still needs looking after. Don't be alone too long."

Grímr glanced back at him once, and Aiden was certain he saw pain in those eyes before Grímr swung onto his horse and turned it away from the other two men, riding off down the coast. Einarr didn't speak or move until Grímr was out of sight. Then, he dropped to his knees beside Aiden to hug the smaller man again, pressing kisses to the top of his head.

"Thank all the gods you're okay," he said, voice shaking. "I thought I'd lost you forever. I'm so sorry, Aiden. If I'd fought harder— I should never have let him even see you, let alone put his hands on you. Please, forgive me."

"There's nothing to forgive," Aiden hushed the other man with a swift, tender kiss. "I wanted to fight. I wouldn't give up being able to fight beside you for anything. Besides, he didn't hurt me. I'm fine, and I'm here with you again. Everything is fine."

Einarr looked doubtful, but he didn't say anything, just held Aiden tightly for another few long moments. It had been just past dawn when they woke, the sky gray and cold. The surf rolled peacefully against the sand, a dull soothing roar behind them.

"What took you so long?" Aiden asked playfully, nudging Einarr's shoulder. "For a moment, I was afraid you weren't coming after me at all."

"I would have torn the world apart just for the chance to see your face again," Einarr responded with such soft sincerity that Aiden's heart skipped a beat.

"I was injured in the raid and unconscious for days. It took me some time to catch up. But I never would have stopped, even if he'd taken you out of Midgard entirely. I would have chased after you right into the underworld if that was where you went. Nothing could ever have stopped me."

Aiden kissed Einarr again, longer this time, letting the other man push him down into the sand. After so long apart, he was aching for Einarr's touch. But the warrior hesitated, his hands beneath Aiden's shirt.

"We don't have time," he sighed reluctantly. "We need to get ahead of Hallvaror's army."

"The boat will take us around the coast faster than they can move over land," Aiden said, fighting the urge to insist Einarr take him now. "It should only take a day or two."

"Then we should get going." Einarr sat up, then bent to carefully sweep Aiden into his arms. "The sooner I get you home and into my bed, the better."

Aiden laughed, feeling as always that there was nowhere he felt safer or more loved that when he was held in Einarr's powerful arms. But somehow, as Einarr loaded him into the boat along with the remaining supplies from Einarr's horse, which he'd released before crossing through the camp, Aiden couldn't stop looking the way Grímr had left, wondering if the other man would really be alright on his own.

Einarr pushed the small boat out into the waves, steering it deftly as they moved out past the breakers.

Einarr kept them a good distance from the shore, not wanting to be spotted if Hallvaror's army wandered too close to the coast. Once, early in the day when they passed a relatively flat area, they saw the army in the distance behind them, moving like a cloud shadow over the land. Aiden quietly wished the waves would carry them faster.

As the day wore on, Aiden noticed a shadow on the hill behind them. Not the army, just a single horse. He said nothing, but somehow he was certain Einarr saw it and knew what it was. They both let it pass unremarked upon.

"That patch," Aiden asked later, wondering about the dark fabric hiding one of Einarr's eyes, "Is that the injury that delayed you?"

Einarr nodded, seemingly untroubled, though Aiden could tell from his stiffness that the man was insecure.

"I lost it," he replied with an offhanded tone. "There'll be an ugly scar as well. You may not think I'm so handsome once we get home."

"As though I fell in love with you for your looks," Aiden laughed, and Einarr looked back to smile at him gently. Aiden leaned forward to touch Einarr's cheek affectionately.

"I thought you were beautiful from the first moment I saw you," he said, "And I will still think so even if you lose your other eye and your nose, as well."

Einarr held Aiden's hand to his cheek, eyes full of love, and Aiden wished again that they were not in

126

such a hurry when all he wanted was to hold the other man.

He glimpsed the rider several more times throughout the day, keeping pace with them, but clearly endeavoring to stay out of sight, though it was a nearly impossible task. Still, he said nothing and neither did Einarr.

Night fell and the waves became too rough to sail safely. Einarr, with clear reluctance, pulled their boat into a sheltered beach.

"We're well ahead of the army," he reassured Aiden. "We can afford to rest for the night. I know how hard Grímr must have been pushing you to stay ahead of me."

"I'm fine," Aiden promised. "I rode mostly, because of the leg, so I'm not too tired. Grímr didn't want to hurt me."

Einarr snorted in disbelief as he built them a small fire and spread a fur on the sand.

"Now that, I have trouble believing. He was desperate to kill you during the raid."

"You saw how quickly he abandoned that plan," Aiden said, sitting in the sand where Einarr had left him when he'd carried the smaller man off the boat. "As soon as he saw he could kidnap me."

"Grímr never was the best at planning," Einarr muttered, fussing with his flint. "Always just ran with whatever he was feeling at the moment. I guess, in spite of everything, that much never changed."

Aiden was quiet for a moment, thoughtful.

"You could have killed him when you were fighting," he said. "More than once, I saw you ignore a fatal blow. It wasn't just today that you couldn't do it."

"I should have," Einarr said guiltily. "Even if I couldn't kill him before, I should have killed him for taking you."

"Why?" Aiden asked curiously. "Why couldn't you kill him?"

Einarr didn't answer at first, prodding at the fire to help it grow, and for a moment, Aiden thought he wouldn't answer at all.

"I loved him once," Einarr confessed, looking away. "We grew up together. He was more than a brother to me. And as we got older, those feelings grew with us. When I saw him again after so long... I couldn't bring myself to hurt him, not even when I could see he was trying to kill me."

The revelation caught Aiden off guard. He supposed he'd always assumed Einarr had other lovers before him. He had a daughter, after all. But it wasn't something he'd ever really thought about. He realized he wasn't jealous, just strangely sad that their relationship had ended in such a way.

"He mentioned you grew up together," Aiden said as Einarr brushed the sand from his clothes, picked Aiden up, and set him on the fur. "What happened between you? How did things end up like this?"

Einarr looked away guiltily, but Aiden pulled the other man down to lay beside him on the fur.

"It won't change how I feel about you," Aiden promised. "Nothing ever could."

"I'm not so sure about that." Einarr ran his hand over Aiden's side, eyes still averted. "What I did... I'm not proud of it. No one would be. If it was known... I would likely be outlawed as well. As a coward."

Aiden's eyes widened, surprised by Einarr's certainty and by the remote and, to him, absurd possibility that Einarr might ever be accused of cowardice.

Aiden reached up to stroke Einarr's cheek, wanting to reassure himself as much as the other man.

"Nothing," he said firmly, "could ever make me love you less. Whatever happened, it was in the past. Before I knew you, before you became the man that I love. It might as well have been done by a stranger."

"But you still want to know," Einarr pointed out, pulling the fur over Aiden's shoulders to keep him warm. "You would still ask me why."

"I want to understand him," Aiden explained. "Why he would hate you so much. It didn't seem in his nature. He was kind, under all that wildness."

"You would not have recognized him back then," Einarr said, his eyes distant. "He was not that wild and desperate creature. He was always a little rougher than others, a little feral, but not like that. Lowborn, and his parents died early. He more or less raised himself. We met as children, not old enough to know how different our destinies were, and remained friends all those years, until we were old enough to go

129

raiding. Old enough to begin thinking about wives. Be neither of us had ever had much eye for women, only each other. We were lovers soon, exploring each other in the loft of my father's barn, learning all the little joys and heartbreaks of first love. We were so caught up in each other, we hardly noticed the world moving on without us."

Einarr's face was lined with sadness as he remembered those distant days, a kind of warm, regretful nostalgia in his eyes. Aiden lay beside him, just listening, stroking the other man's hand as he talked.

"My family was wealthy, well-respected," he said, "And powerful. And soon, it began to be suggested that I should marry the daughter of another powerful family. Her name was Snotra and she was as fair and talented and honorable as any man could hope for. I was proud to be chosen for her. But my ties to Grímr held me back. I knew if I married her, whatever else happened, I would never be free to be with Grímr again. Grímr accepted it. He was ready to let me go. He'd always been waiting for it, I think. For our destinies to pull us apart. But I was young and spoiled and unused to not getting what I wanted."

He hesitated, looking down at Aiden, the love in his eyes tinged with worry.

"You're certain," he asked, eyes drawn in worry, "Nothing could change your feelings for me?"

"Of course," Aiden assured him. Part of him knew he should say that Einarr didn't have to tell him this story, that he could wait as long as it took for

Einarr to be comfortable sharing this with him. But he wanted to know. He couldn't stop the burn of his curiosity demanding more.

"I went to Snotra," Einarr continued, uneasy, "And I confessed that I couldn't marry her. That I didn't want to. She pressed me for answers, hurt and angry. I told her I loved someone else, but she wanted a name. And I told her. I confessed that I could never love her, because I was in love with Grímr. She laughed at me first, then grew offended, thinking I was mocking her, suggesting anyone would rather have a man than her. And when I continued to insist that I loved him, she grew angry and said she refused to be shamed in this way. She would tell everyone of my weakness, my cowardice, in submitting to another man. It is one thing for a thrall, or even a freedman, to submit to his master. This is expected. But for someone like me to surrender to someone like Grímr... They might have outlawed us both. I certainly would have lost everything. She was not a bad person. I'm not trying to excuse my actions. She was as kind and dutiful as anyone. We're all capable of cruelty when we're angry and ashamed. Perhaps if I had not done what I did then, she never would have told my secret at all."

He paused again, his hand almost painfully tight where he held Aiden's, his eyes far away and full of guilt.

"She struck me and, in my fear and my rage, I fought with her," he said, and Aiden, beginning to sense where this was going, felt his heartbeat

131

quicken. "It is not a moment I remember well. She stumbled, I think. I hope she stumbled. She hit her head and it was over in a moment, her blood still warm on my hands."

Aiden had seen it coming, but he still shuddered, horrified at the thought of Einarr killing a woman in anger. And he knew he couldn't hope to understand how much worse such a crime was for the Northmen, for whom there were few sins more unforgivable.

"I fled," Einarr went on, and Aiden wondered how much worse it could get. "I ran to Grímr, who I knew would protect me. And he did, more than I could have asked for. Those that had guessed at our relationship accused Grímr of being the murderer. And Grímr, unwilling to incriminate me, confessed. He stood in the great hall before the Jarl and told them he loved me, and that I'd never accepted him. He said he'd killed Snotra for taking what he could never have. He never flinched. He took their hate and their judgement and their abuse like wind throwing itself against a mountain. And when they sentenced him to outlawry, all his rights and property stripped, banished to the wilds, every man living forbidden from giving him aid, he asked me to come with him. In the wild, we could have been together with no one to tell us that our love made us cowards."

Aiden felt his heart sink with shame, for he knew he could not have gone to join the other man.

"The night he was driven from town," Einarr said, "Arnnjorn came to me. He was childless and widowed and, knowing the ridicule I would face in Ingifast for my connection to the scandal, he offered that I should come and live in Arnnstead with him. My parents accepted for me. I could have escaped. I could have run away any hundred times and gone to find Grímr. But I was afraid, and it was easier to tell myself I was trapped and had no choice. I left Ingifast. I let Grímr take the punishment for my crime, and then I ran away and never saw him again. That's why he hates me. That's why he has every right to hate me. I'm a coward, and I abandoned him."

For a moment, Aiden could only stare, overwhelmed by what he had learned. Einarr looked away, closing his eyes, his features lined heavy with shame. But then Aiden shook it off, touching Einarr's cheek.

"No," he insisted fiercely, "You're not a coward. I've seen you fight. I've seen you risk death to defend what you love. Whatever you were then, you are not anymore. That person is gone. The Einarr I know is kind and gentle and brave. He rode for days to find me, injured and not knowing if I was even alive, or if he might be running into a trap. He would rather lose an eye than strike down a man he once loved. He told me this story, even when he was certain I would no longer love him by the end of it, rather than deny me. The Einarr I love, the Einarr in front of me now, is the bravest man I know."

Tears rolled from beneath the cloth over Einarr's eye, and he trembled with relief as he pulled Aiden close. Aiden kissed the other man hard, all the love he'd been holding back for days spilling out at once. Einarr returned it, and the warmth of his tongue turned the love of that kiss into the heat of desire. His hand slid down to cup Aiden's backside. He pressed a thigh between the smaller man's legs, and Aiden groaned into the kiss as he rocked against that pressure, suddenly needy for more. It felt like it had been ages. Einarr seemed to be feeling similarly hungry, his free hand tangling in Aiden's hair to keep him close, fingernails scraping his scalp. Aiden rode Einarr's thigh shamelessly, though it made his injured leg twinge. He'd been missing this too long to care. He'd been missing Einarr too long to care. Just being this close to him again was driving Aiden wild. The familiar scent of him, the touch of his hands, the taste of his lips. Aiden wanted to be immersed in it forever.

The ocean roared behind them, drowning out the sound of their labored breathing as Einarr rolled Aiden onto his back and shifted over him, allowing Aiden to better rest his leg as the warrior moved between his thighs, tugging his leggings down as far as he could without having to pull them over the troublesome makeshift splint. Aiden, suddenly exposed, was too aware of the night air on his skin, the cool ocean breeze, stirring the delicate red curls above his manhood. They'd never done it outside before, and it left Aiden feeling flustered and vulnerable. As much as he knew they were miles from anything, he couldn't help worrying someone would stumble across them. If anyone but Einarr saw him like this, he thought he'd die of embarrassment.

He was quickly distracted from his worries by Einarr's warm fingers wrapping around his shaft. He inhaled sharply, covering his mouth to stifle a cry, but Einarr pulled Aiden's hand away a moment later.

"I want to hear your voice," he said. His voice rough with desire. "There's no one to hear you out here. You don't need to hold back. I want to hear you shouting my name."

Just hearing those words was enough to bring a needy moan from Aiden. It just wasn't fair of the older man to say things like that.

A moment later, Aiden had ample reason to make plenty of noise as Einarr's tongue, hot and wet, dragged up the underside of his cock. Aiden gasped the other man's name, his hips lifting to follow that contact, his hands gripping Einarr's shoulders. It always left him paralyzed with embarrassment whenever Einarr did this, which he thought was half the reason Einarr liked doing it so much. The man had never been quiet about how much he enjoyed Aiden's lewd expressions.

Einarr wrapped his mouth around Aiden's head, and before Aiden could so much as brace himself, plunged, taking Aiden nearly to the hilt and surrounding him in tight heat that left his head spinning, stammering Einarr's name as his toes curled in the sand. Einarr's mouth moved over him in smooth passes, leaving him wet in the cold air when the heat of Einarr's lips retreated, only to return a moment later in a startling swipe of tongue across Aiden's entrance. Aiden gasped, blushing all the way to his

135

ears at the thought of Einarr doing something so dirty, but he could do little more than stammer helpless protests as Einarr teased him mercilessly, tongue squirming against Aiden's hole while Einarr's hand stroked his shaft.

All too soon, Einarr pulled away, leaving Aiden's entrance tingling in his wake, to fumble through their bags impatiently for a jar of oil. Aiden felt a rush of excitement and nerves as he realized what Einarr was planning. The older man's mouth engulfed him again a moment later, but his fingers, slick with oil, were pressing below, opening Aiden up with steady, insistent touches. Aiden trembled as Einarr's fingers curled within him at the same moment the other man's mouth swept down to swallow Aiden to the root.

Being stimulated in both places at once was almost too much to bear. Aiden writhed under Einarr's careful attention, but the warrior always kept him just on the edge of completion, pulling back just when Aiden thought he was finished. At last, when Aiden thought he could take no more and Einarr's fingers had him well prepared, Einarr suddenly redoubled his efforts, tongue lashing the base of Aiden's cock, fingers curling inside to press against Aiden's inner walls in a way that made Aiden delirious with pleasure. The crashing of waves mirrored the white noise that filled his ears as a long awaited orgasm rolled over him and he spilled himself in Einarr's mouth.

Einarr milked him dry before he pulled away, licking his lips, in order to look down on Aiden, no doubt enjoying the flustered mess he'd left his lover in. Aiden just lay dazed, trying to catch his breath, hands knotted in the fur beneath him and the smell of salt spray baffling his senses. Before he could recover, he felt pressure at his entrance, realizing Einarr had moved over him. He held his breath as he felt Einarr sliding into him, slowly spreading him open. Aiden would never get over how good it felt just to feel Einarr inside him. The weight of it, the fullness. There was no better feeling in the world than lying beneath the man he loved. It was so much more than just the raw pleasure, though that was fantastic too. It was the intimacy of being so close to another person. Of trusting Einarr enough to see him this way and never hurt him. By all the pagan gods, he had missed this man.

Einarr rolled his hips slowly, keeping beat with the ocean as he surged into Aiden. Every stroke filled Aiden with heat and growing desire. Though he'd only come recently, Einarr's steady pace, relentless as the sea, soon stirred him to arousal again. Only then did Einarr increase his pace. Aiden hooked his good leg around the other man's back to urge him on, and Einarr ground deeper into him in response, making Aiden moan. Soon, the warrior was striking Aiden like hammer blows, his body quaking with every hit. Aiden shook with desire, head tipping back as he clutched Einarr's shoulders for stability.

And there, on the hill beyond the beach, just beyond where Aiden could see clearly, he saw a man looking down at them. He didn't question for a second who it was. Einarr, unaware, swore as Aiden suddenly tightened around him. The thought of Grímr watching them made Aiden's stomach squirm with butterflies. What was he thinking from his place up there on the hill? Did he hate Aiden for sharing so eagerly with Einarr what he'd refused the outlaw? Did he hate Einarr more than ever? Or was he only wishing he could be in the warrior's place?

Before he could stop himself, Aiden imagined Grímr leaning over him, moving inside him. Heat and excitement thrummed through him, mingling with guilt that he would think of another man while he was with Einarr. But his fantasies ran wild within him, imagining Grímr coming down the hill to join them. Imagining him kissing Einarr, the two of them touching each other. Touching Aiden. What would it feel like to be pressed between the two of them, touched on all sides until he was so overwhelmed he—

Einarr had only just reached to touch Aiden's need, but the barest brush of his fingers followed by the surge of his cock against Aiden's deepest places was all Aiden needed. He came, shuddering and gasping Einarr's name, though his head still swam with images of the outlaw and the warrior taking him together. He tightened around Einarr, who cursed and pulled Aiden close as he thrust in as deeply as he could to leave his seed within the younger man.

Their skin cooled in the evening air as they lay together, still joined, waiting for their breathing to return to normal and the glow of pleasure to fade. Aiden kept glancing up the hill, but Grímr had vanished again, and Aiden could only guess at his motivations. He didn't know why the man was still following them in the first place.

He slept curled up against Einarr's chest, feeling certain there was no other place he'd rather be. But sleep didn't come easily. His eyes scanned the hills, wondering if Grímr was there, or making camp somewhere nearby, sleepless and watching the hills the same as Aiden was. For a moment, he was struck by a wild impulse to leave Einarr sleeping and go find the outlaw. To do what, he wasn't sure. Tell him to leave? Or ask him to join them? Or maybe...

He looked up at Einarr's face and felt no doubt that he loved the man. Their relationship was still young, but it had been tested powerfully, and they'd come through it still together. Aiden didn't have to wonder whether he would die for the man he loved. He knew the answer because he'd already risked his life a dozen times for that very reason. And yet, insecurity remained. The difficulties of finding his place in a culture so different from the one he had been born in. Trying to get along with people, many of them as close to Einarr as family, who looked at Aiden with disdain or openly mocked him for being born on a different shore and for taking the woman's part in bed. And always the creeping worry that one day Einarr would get tired of him. Tire of the 'playful' jokes from the other men, the disappointed tutting of the women. Tire of how clueless Aiden was about every aspect of life here. Of his insecurity, his temper, his pointless bickering when he was bored or nervous or frustrated. He would get tired of Aiden one day, Aiden was sure of it, and the thought made him feel almost nauseous with dismay. What would happen when Einarr was through with him? He had nowhere else to go. Would he stay in that house, doing chores, caring for Einarr's daughter, as the warrior brought home someone else?

He could feel himself sinking into a cycle of useless worries, and he shook them off quickly. There was no point in being afraid of a future he had no guarantee would ever happen. It was better to focus on the present— the immediate danger presented by Hallvaror's army. He would worry about the future when it happened. What else could he do, after all?

Chapter Twelve

They woke shortly after sunrise the next morning and took to their boat again, resuming their sail down the coast. Aiden knew they'd left the army far behind them, but he still wished they could move faster. Who knew what damage Hallvaror might do before they could get warnings to all the villages in his path?

Grímr was still following them. Aiden glimpsed the distant shadow of the horseman on the hill again and again throughout the day. He was certain Einarr saw it too. Aiden wondered what the outlaw could be planning and quietly worried.

They stopped again that night, and again Grímr did not approach. Aiden lay in Einarr's arms, wondering if the outlaw was watching, what he might be thinking. At last, he gave up on waiting. He slid carefully out of slumbering Einarr's embrace and reached for his pine branch crutch. Einarr had stripped the last of the dried twigs and bark off of it and made it a proper walking stick, though he kept insisting Aiden should not be walking at all. Aiden was too anxious to sit still.

He climbed the beach, his stick sliding in the sand and on the rocky shore. On the hill above the sea where the tall grass waved in the night breeze, he stood pale illuminated by the moon and scanned the land below for some sign of Grímr. As though he'd been waiting, the outlaw stepped out of the shadows, approaching Aiden silently.

"Come to take me away again?" Aiden asked with quiet humor.

"Only if you want you me to," Grímr replied with no humor at all, and Aiden's heart ached in response.

"Have you been taking care of that wound?" he asked. "Let me see it."

He sat down in the tall grass, and Grímr sat beside him, letting Aiden tend his injuries as he had before. For a time, they were quiet, each waiting on the other to say what they'd come there to say.

"Why are you following us?"

It was Aiden who broke first as he was re-bandaging Grímr's injury.

"Einarr gave you the chance to be free," Aiden frowned, looking up at the outlaw in concern. "You could have gone anywhere. Why are you risking your life to come after us? Do you still want your revenge on him that badly?"

"No," Grímr admitted. "No, it's not about revenge anymore."

"Then what is it about?" Aiden insisted, but Grímr wouldn't answer or meet his eye.

"I don't want to see you killed." Aiden reached for Grímr's hand, wanting the other man to understand him. "For my sake if nothing else, you have to give up on revenge. Find another way to live."

Grímr was quiet for a long moment.

"Why couldn't it be me?" he asked at last. "If you can still love him, even with all he's done, why couldn't you learn to love me?"

Aiden pursed his lips, looking away. The truth was that he could, possibly already had. But he couldn't give up Einarr. Even if Grímr was looking at him right now like a drowning man looking toward land.

"You've been alone too long," Aiden answered at last. "I'm not that special. If you leave this country, you'll find a hundred fair men and women eager to love you."

"None like you," Grímr said, and his touch grazed Aiden's cheek like the brush of a moth's wing. "None with half your grace. None who would heal the

142

wounds of a man who threatened to kill them. None who would stand between that man and the sword of their own lover and plead for their enemy's life. I'm certain there's no other man like you in all of creation."

Aiden trembled, hearing the devotion in Grímr's voice, his insecurities rising again, wondering if it wouldn't be wiser to leave now, before Einarr had a chance to realize how much better he could do. Grímr leaned in closer and Aiden turned away, his heart undecided, and Grímr pressed a kiss to his cheek instead.

"I'll follow you," Grímr said, "To the ends of the earth. To my death, if that's what the gods have decided. I won't force you, won't speak a word in your direction if you don't will it. But if you ever change your mind, I will be only over the next hill, waiting for you."

Aiden looked away toward the waning moon, his jaw set.

"Is it really me you're following?" he asked quietly, "Or is it him you can't give up on?"

Grímr didn't answer, his face cast in shadow as a cloud covered the moon.

"You spent twenty years obsessing over him. It's hardly surprising that there are still feelings there."

"I could forget him," Grímr protested, "For you."

Somehow, Aiden knew that was a lie. He had a feeling Grímr did too.

Aiden stood, unwilling to look at the other man.

"You should leave." He turned and began hobbling back toward to beach. "You deserve better than waiting on me. Go find somewhere you can be happy."

Grímr didn't answer, and Aiden refused to look back to see his face, but somehow, he knew Grímr wasn't going to give up so easily.

He crawled back into the furs next to Einarr, and wasn't surprised to find the other man lying awake. Einarr didn't ask, and when Aiden put his arms around the other man to cling to him, trembling, Einarr only squeezed him tightly, rubbing his back in quiet reassurance.

Chapter Thirteen

By the next day, the first of the coastal towns was in sight. They docked their boat briefly and spoke with the chief. Einarr's reputation was enough to get them a meeting, and he vouched for Aiden's story.

"If what you say is true," the town's grizzled chief replied, "Then Hallvaror is a coward. Only the worst kind of scum could murder his own father in such an underhanded way. If his bannermen knew, they would sooner die than follow him. I'll prepare my town, but I also intend to send messages to the other chiefs and the jarls of the northern clans. If a ting— a meeting of the jarls— is called, it will at the very least cast doubt on Hallvaror's leadership. His army will be forced to halt until a verdict is reached. If nothing else, it could buy us valuable time."

"Then I'll tell all the other villages to do the same," Einarr agreed. "Such a dishonorable man should never be allowed to rule such an army."

They moved on, stopping at every village they passed. Many requested they stay to eat and drink, but the message they carried was too urgent. In many villages, they encountered doubt, even hostility. Hallvaror was a powerful warrior, a hero, well-respected. The kind of man sagas were written about. It was hard for some to believe he was capable of such a thing. Though Aiden's frustration tended to lead him to snap at people in frustration, Einarr was patient, keeping Aiden in check while he persuaded those he could to prepare themselves, even if they chose not to help.

It was well past dark when Aiden recognized the familiar sight of Arnnstead before them.

"We're home," he said, relieved, and Einarr smiled at him, tired but equally grateful to be back.

Though they both longed to go to their beds, they headed for the longhouse instead, where the people had gathered for the evening meal. A hush fell over the hall as Einarr stepped inside, supporting Aiden, who limped at his side. The hush soon became a cheer, shouts of Einarr's name bringing Arnnjorn from the other end of the hall. Still weak from his injuries, he nonetheless hugged Einarr so tightly that the younger man's feet left the ground.

"It's good to see you too, Aiden!" Arnnjorn put Einarr down to pat Aiden's shoulder heavily. "I saw how fiercely you fought in the raid. I knew you would not be stolen away so easily. They are calling you Broken-Shield now, for how you defended Einarr with your shield split down the middle."

"I suppose I'm lucky they aren't calling me Aiden the Kidnapped," Aiden laughed, then wobbled unsteadily, leaning on Einarr.

"We should get you to a healer," Arnnjorn frowned, reaching out to steady the smaller man. "Someone call for Yrsa!"

"Wait," Aiden caught Arnnjorn's hand to support himself, "Not yet, we have important news. There's danger—"

"I'll tell him," Einarr promised. "You go and rest. That leg has been neglected far too long. Unless you want them to change your name to Aiden the Lame?"

Aiden reluctantly accepted their concern, and when Yrsa arrived, he let her lead him away to a quieter place where he could lay down as she tended his broken leg.

"It was set well," she reported, "And it doesn't appear diseased."

Aiden hadn't seen under the bandage and splint in a while. Near the break, his skin was an angry, swollen red. Yrsa thumped the red skin, sending a jolt of searing pain through him. He couldn't even yell, just fall back gasping and wheezing.

"You've been walking on it," Yrsa observed. "You've made it much worse than it should have been. You're not allowed to set one foot on the ground till this swelling has gone down."

She wrapped the break in a poultice that cooled the inflamed skin and soothed the pain, then left him to rest. At first, he fidgeted, considering ignoring her orders in order to go back to the longhouse and check on things with Einarr, but to be honest, he was more than a little frightened of Yrsa. He didn't want to upset her. And the longer he lay there, the more comfortable the bed began to feel. It had been a little while since he'd slept on one of the fur-lined benches the Northmen favored. They were certainly better than the ground. Soon, his eyes began to close and he drifted off into exhausted sleep.

He woke the next morning to the sound of Einarr arguing with Yrsa.

"He can rest just as well at home, in his own bed."

"You've been letting him wander over half of Midgard on that leg! I don't trust you to let him rest for a minute."

"Jódís will be there to look after him, and he'll be more comfortable there than cooped up in this shed."

"I don't care about his comfort; I care about his health!"

"Do I get a say in this?" Aiden asked, sitting up and rubbing his eyes.

Yrsa was standing near the door of the little house, glaring at Einarr, who stood on the other side of it, obviously trying to shoulder his way inside. Yrsa sniffed.

"Of course," she said reluctantly. "It is your decision."

"Then I'd like to go home," he replied. "I've been away too long."

Einarr smiled, and Yrsa begrudgingly let him pass. He scooped Aiden up at once, careful of his leg, and pressed a discrete kiss to the top of Aiden's head.

"Then let's go home."

He carried Aiden the whole way back, which Aiden appreciated for multiple reasons, not the least of which was how many people wanted to stop and congratulate he and Einarr both on the ferocity they'd displayed during the raid. It seemed so far away now that Aiden hardly knew how to respond. He was used to these people tolerating him with a kind of derogatory amusement. This sudden respect confused him. They hadn't been this gracious even after he'd helped defend the village last winter and earned his release from thralldom. He supposed raiding was a different kind of honor. Maybe things would be better now? He could hardly dare to hope. If their acceptance faded as it had in the months following winter, he wondered if he would have gained any ground at all.

It was good to be back home, regardless of anything else. Agna and Jódís were happier to see him again than Aiden had expected. Jódís had always been a little cool toward him, disapproving of Aiden's relationship with her brother. But she hugged him when she saw him alive, and fussed over his injury like a mother, which pleased Aiden more than he expected it to. Einarr received an even more substantial amount of fussing, which Aiden supported. He still felt guilty that Einarr had lost an eye and he hadn't been there to help. But for Einarr and the other warriors, it seemed to be more of a badge of honor than a loss. Only Jódís seemed upset with it.

"It's such a shame," she muttered. "You were so handsome."

"I think I'm still handsome, thank you!" Einarr scoffed, playing more offended than he was. Aiden, with Agna on his lap, laughed.

"Aiden! Tell her I'm still handsome!" Einarr demanded playfully.

"Well, I'll say I don't think your level of attractiveness has changed much at all," Aiden conceded, then winked at Agna. "I always thought you were ugly."

This brought laughter and agreement from the women, and a theatrical wounded cry from Einarr.

"So, what is this news you brought to Arnnjorn?" Jódís asked later as they ate together. "And what's being done about it? I hear Jarl Bjorn has been murdered by his own son."

"That's the truth of it," Einarr confirmed. "Aiden saw it happen. Jarl Bjorn was gathering his armies. He and Hallvaror fought over whether they should take a fleet raiding in Vinland or conquer the coastal villages. Then Hallvaror put a knife in Bjorn's back. I can't imagine what he's told his army, but now he's leading them toward the coast."

"So, what is Arnnjorn going to do about it?" Jódís asked, and Aiden leaned forward, equally curious to hear what had happened.

"The other village chiefs are trying to call a ting," Einarr explained. "Arnnjorn supports it. Bring Hallvaror's fellow Jarls down on him for this cowardly behavior. In the meantime, the plan is to bring together all the men of the coastal villages and try to build a force that can at least slow Hallvaror's army down. With any luck, we won't have to use it."

"With any luck, the gods will strike Hallvaror down himself for such an act, and for squandering all the gifts he was blessed with," Jódís added. "I still

150

can't believe he would do such a thing. You're certain it was as you saw, Aiden?"

"Absolutely," Aiden confirmed. "I saw it with my own eyes. Hallvaror is a murderer. He's convinced that, if he doesn't unite the north, then the English will overtake us."

"He's a young fool, too ambitious for his own good," Einarr added. "With a little more age and wisdom, he might have grown to be a great leader. The impatience of youth is a destructive thing."

"So, what happens next?" Aiden asked, turning to Einarr. "What should I do?"

"What happens next for you is that you rest," Einarr said firmly. "Yrsa said you aren't to put any weight on that leg for a month, at least. Tomorrow, chieftains from all the nearby villages will begin gathering in Arnnjorn's hall. In a few days, when they're all assembled, a meeting will be held to decide our strategy."

"And I'll be there, right?" Aiden asked, suddenly worried. "I was the one that saw it happen."

"You will be right here, not moving that leg." Einarr shook a finger at Aiden, his eyes firm as stone. "If they need to hear the story again, I will tell it."

"But you didn't see it," Aiden blustered, suddenly protective of his achievement, however dubious, perhaps hoping further glory would further endear him to the town and assure his place here. "I want to be the one that tells them."

"I'm sorry, Aiden." Einarr was as stubborn and immovable as a mountain. "You will not be attending that meeting, if I have stay here and sit on you myself to keep you from going."

If it were not for how recently he'd been reminded of his love for the man, Aiden might have stayed in a sulk for days at such treatment. As it was, he only gave Einarr the cold shoulder for a night, then began plotting how to attend the meeting anyway.

A few days later, all the men and the leaders of the coastal villages were gathered in the longhouse.

Einarr tugged on his nicest wolf pelt cloak to look as impressive as he could, then bent and kissed Aiden on the forehead. Jódís and Agna were off with the other women, weaving within easy listening distance of the hall, participating whether they were asked to or not.

"There will be drinking and feasting after," he said, "So I'll be back late. Try to behave yourself. If I get back and find out you've been wandering about—"

"I'm not going to wander." Aiden rolled his eyes. "Do you think I enjoy walking on a broken leg? Go enjoy your stupid meeting, then."

"I know you wanted to be there," Einarr took Aiden's hands, "But rest assured, you will be honored for what you did. I'll make certain of it. So just stay here and be patient for now."

Aiden nodded reluctantly, and Einarr smiled.

"I love you." The older man's voice ached with tender sincerity, and Aiden couldn't help warming to it.

"I love you too," he said, letting his put-out expression melt so that he could lean up and kiss the other man. "Hurry back."

Einarr turned to leave, then paused, turned back, and snatched Aiden's pine walking stick from beside the bed.

"Taking this," he declared as he hurried out the door, "Just in case."

"What? Don't you dare!"

But the door had already slammed shut behind Einarr. Aiden slumped back onto the bench with a hiss of frustration. There went a good half of his plans. Einarr knew him entirely too well.

Aiden wondered if Einarr would take the walking stick all the way to the hall with him or just leave it outside. Was it worth dragging himself to the door to find out? Maybe it would be better to just do as Einarr said and stay put. But he wanted to be at that meeting! Even Agna was getting to listen in. It wasn't fair to expect him to stay here.

He scooted to the end of the bench and swung his legs over, but didn't stand yet, making a clumsy swipe for the nearby fire poker. Maybe he could use that as a temporary crutch until he got to the door. After a few frustrating swipes and nearly knocking the damn thing into the embers where he'd have no chance of recovering it, he managed to get a grip on it and drag it closer.

He quickly realized it was far too short for a walking stick. How bent over he'd have to be in order to use it made it practically useless. At least it was something to steady himself on as he clung to the wall and stumbled between the house's supporting pillars, doing his best not to put any weight on his injured leg. After what felt like forever and an endless count of bruises on his shoulders from colliding with pillars, he made it the front door and carefully pushed it open, struggling not to fall out with it. The early summer day was hot and humid outside, not a breeze stirring through the village streets. There was no sign of his walking stick on either side of the door. Aiden cursed and contemplated the walk to Arnnjorn's hall. Einarr's house was at the furthest end of the village, nearest the bathing springs, but a fair distance from everything else, including the hall. It was not, Aiden decided, a walk he could manage. Probably not even with the stick, to be honest, but without it, he decided it wasn't worth even attempting. With a string of bitter curses, he limped back inside and closed the door behind him, making his slow, uncomfortable way back to his bench. He really didn't have any choice but just to wait. Frustrated indignation gnawed at him, but he swallowed it, laying back on the bench and reaching for one of his carving projects instead.

Aiden's wood carving was what had first caught Einarr's eye. The brief connection they'd made, trading for one of Aiden's carvings, was what had saved Aiden later when the Vikings had raided his village. Now, he carved dragons on the prows of their ships. Faralder, who was the village carpenter, had been teaching Aiden a great deal about carving. Aiden was still learning, but he appreciated the tangled intricacy of the Northmen's style. The only thing that bothered him was how utilitarian they were about their art. They'd put all manner of flourishes on weapons and tools and boats, but they made nothing simply for the sake of being beautiful. Everything needed to be useful as well as lovely. It frustrated him when he wanted to make something and Faralder clicked his tongue and demanded to know what purpose it would serve. The purpose of Aiden enjoying making it was apparently not good enough.

At least at home Einarr indulged him, letting him carve whatever he liked in his free time. He'd made a host of useless little trinkets to amuse Agna and decorate the house. Since he'd returned, he'd started working on something new. It was more complicated than what he usually did, but the image had refused to leave him until he'd tried his hand at realizing it. It was a battle scene, a great horned stag, proud and mighty, tangled in conflict with a wolf, ragged and starving, its eyes gleaming with hunger and its teeth bared. It looked to all appearances like the stag was winning, but Aiden wondered if the wolf might take them both down when he went. Aiden wasn't skilled enough to do justice to what he saw in his mind, but he tried regardless, sculpting away at it slowly over the days he'd been trapped in bed.

A knock on the door, loud and demanding, made his hand slip, nicking his thumb.

"Who is it?" Aiden called, putting his carving aside and leaning off his bench. "I can't come to the door!"

"Aiden Broken-Shield?" a man called. "Your testimony is needed in the hall."

"What?" Aiden, confused, swung his legs over the bench and tried to stand, "I thought Einarr was—"

"The chiefs want you there."

"Well I can't walk, so—"

The door swung open so abruptly that Aiden jumped and reached for his knife instinctively. He didn't recognize the men that entered and came toward him.

"Hold on just a minute." Aiden gripped his knife. "If you want me there, go and get Einarr to bring me. I'm not supposed to walk on this leg, or I'll end up lame— hey!"

Rather than answering, the two men disarmed Aiden with apparent ease and grabbed him under the arms, lifting him up so that his feet barely skimmed the ground. They carried him out like that despite his protests, dangling between them like a prisoner. Aiden's head spun with confusion.

They reached the hall, and the men marched Aiden in without hesitation.

"Ah, here he is now." A short, red-bearded man was standing at the end of the hall before the chair where Arnnjorn set, the other chiefs around him. "This is the source whose honor Arnnjorn claims is so unquestionable."

The two men carrying Aiden threw him down before the chiefs, and he cried out in pain as his leg hit the ground, muttering curses in Welsh as pain throbbed through him. What was going on? Where was Einarr?

"An English thrall," the strange man declared loudly, pointing an accusative finger at Aiden. "And one well-known for his effeminate ways. Was there ever a more untrustworthy man in the world? And yet, Arnnjorn would have us believe he is beyond reproach."

"Aiden is not a thrall," Arnnjorn said, his voice calm but threatening in its low rumble. "He's earned his freedom through honorable deeds, defending this village from his own countrymen. His loyalty is not in question. And I would watch who you accuse of argr under this roof Astrader, if you intend to be alive beneath it much longer."

The red-bearded man, Astrader, met Arnnjorn's glare with fearsome stubbornness, but adopted a more diplomatic tone.

"Arnnjorn trusts this creature, clearly," Astrader said to the assembled chiefs, not sparing a glance for Aiden, who still knelt on the floor of the hall, wondering why he was suddenly on trial and where Einarr could have gone. He was meant to be here.

"But are you all willing to risk going to war with Hallvaror on the words of an English *former* thrall? It is the world of Hallvaror, a high born jarl and proven hero, that his father was killed in an honorable battle with men who had come seeking revenge on Bjorn for earlier slights. Men whom Hallvaror himself slayed and whose bodies were seen by many. Would you really take this thing's words over that of a jarl?"

"What reason would he have to lie about such a thing?" Arnnjorn argued. "He gains nothing by it."

"And Hallvaror's strife with his father was well-known," pointed out another chief. "Their arguments could shake the halls. Hallvaror's temper was compared to Thor's. I, for one, do not find it shocking at all that he would attack his father. Only that he would strike from behind with such cowardice."

"Bjorn was still as mighty as he was when we were young men," Arnnjorn said with fond nostalgia in his voice. "He would have defeated Hallvaror in honest combat. And the foolish boy is convinced the future of our people is at stake. He would not risk losing."

"You insult Jarl Bjorn by insinuating he would not have noticed a man so close to him planning his death!" shouted yet another chief. "I tell you, Bjorn would never have fallen so easily!"

"We are often blind to the true intentions of those closest to us," the chief who had spoken before of Hallvaror's temper spoke again. "No man would want to believe his son capable of such a thing. Bjorn was a great jarl, but a man like all of us, and vulnerable to the same follies."

"All of this is beside the point," Arnnjorn cut in. "Hallvaror's guilt or innocence will be decided at the ting. However he came by it, he *is* marching this way with an army, and we must be prepared to face it. Will we scatter and divide to make it easier for him to mow us down? Or will we come together and give him a fight worth having?"

"There is a third option," Astrader declared, drowning out the men agreeing with Arnnjorn's words, "Which is precisely the point I am trying to make. Arnnjorn would have you believe you can only fight or die. He asks what this English thrall would have to gain by turning you against Hallvaror. The answer is keeping us divided! Weak! Fodder for his people, the filthy English, which Hallvaror, with a unified north, would defeat! We have already seen last winter that Arnnjorn would let this hall burn before anyone pried it from his greedy fingers, but are you all so eager to see your homes destroyed? Or would you rather be part of something great? The most powerful army the north has ever seen! A force strong enough to bring not just the English, but the world to its knees!"

There was a thoughtful murmur through the chiefs, and Aiden could only watch, horrified, as he saw more of the chiefs beginning to consider Astrader's words. If that many of them joined Hallvaror, Arnnstead would not have enough men to stand against him.

"I am not a thrall," he shouted, trying to get attention as he struggled, ignoring the pain, onto his feet, "And I am *not* English! My heart is here! My loyalty is here! I've spilled my blood for this place, and it was no different than yours! I saw the coward Hallvaror murder his father, and if you expect him to treat your homes and families with any more honor than he treated his own, if you are given the chance to fight like men and choose to roll over like dogs, then you deserve whatever fate befalls you!

"Still according only to your word!" Astrader said, taking control back before the chiefs could respond to Aiden's impassioned condemnation, "Which cannot be trusted!"

"If there were but one other witness," one of the chiefs muttered, shaking his head.

"There is another."

A voice spoke from the other end of the hall, where a man stood near the doors. He stepped forward as attention was turned his way, and Aiden's breath caught as he recognized the handsome, haggard face beneath the cloak.

"I was there," Grímr declared boldly, moving to Aiden's side. "I saw it too."

"And who are you that we should trust your word any more than his?" Astrader asked skeptically.

"I am Grímr, son of Audgrímr of Ingifast," he said. "My father had no fine titles, but I was free born as any of you. And I too saw the coward Hallvaror murder his own father for the sake of his ambition."

"And how did you come to be there?" Astrader asked, a suspicious glint in his eye. "How did you come to witness this?"

"Because I am the outlaw who stole Aiden from Ingifast during the raid and stole through Bjorn's encampment in the night to reach the coast and flee this country."

He stated it so calmly and so plainly that, for a moment, the entire hall was stunned. A moment later, it erupted into angry shouts, and men rushed forward to catch the unresisting Grímr by his arms.

160

"There you have it," Astrader spat, "A thrall and an outlaw. What better argument could I make that this is lies and trickery?"

Grímr said nothing more, and his eyes never left Aiden's as he was dragged from the suddenly noisy hall. Aiden could only stare after him, wide-eyed and horrified, as the clamor of voices rose around him.

"That proves it's a lie!"

"But why would he break his outlawry and ensure his death for a lie?"

"It's a trick, an English trick!"

"Is that still not enough witnesses to convince you?"

It all became white noise in Aiden's ears. He fell, the pain in his leg too great to go on ignoring, and arms were there to catch him. The familiar scent of Einarr surrounded him, and he breathed it in with a sigh of relief.

"I'm so sorry, Aiden," Einarr spoke, barely audible above the roar of conflicting voices that filled the hall. "I should have been here. I've failed you again. I'm sorry..."

He carried Aiden out of the chaos of the hall, hardly noticed by the still-arguing chiefs. Einarr didn't take Aiden home, but up to the hills above the town, away from the clamor and the oppressive presence of other people. The wind had changed, sweeping down from the mountains and bringing the cool air of their ever-frosted peaks down with it. The summer grasses swayed in the golden light of late afternoon, and the hills were painted with a dozen shades of wild flower.

The peaceful, pastoral scene was entirely at odds with the tempest raging in town, and in Aiden's heart. He almost longed for those days in the cave with Grímr. How simple it had been then, too focused on just staying alive to think of anything else. Once other people became involved, everything became so much more complicated so quickly...

"Where have they taken Grímr?" he asked as Einarr sat beside him in the grass. "Is he dead?"

"He should be," Einarr replied. "He should have been killed on sight for entering any settlement. But with all the confusion, they won't kill him yet. They'll want to keep him as an important witness."

"That's why you wouldn't let me go to the meeting, wasn't it?" Aiden stared out at the hills, wishing they could calm his racing heart. "You and Arnnjorn weren't going to tell them who the witness was. You knew they wouldn't believe it, coming from me."

"Astrader must have discovered it somehow," Einarr confirmed. "He's always been Hallvaror's dog. He knew if I vouched for you, people would believe anyway. He had men corner me on my way to the meeting, claiming raiders had been spotted and I was needed to stand watch. They wouldn't let me leave until Jódís found me. She'd heard you being dragged in and knew something was wrong. If I had gotten away sooner..."

"It's not your fault." Aiden stopped Einarr quickly. "Grímr made his own decision."

"I'm not worried about Grímr," Einarr corrected. "I mean, I am, but I meant you. I should never have let Astrader humiliate you like that in front of everyone."

"It's nothing I'm not used to." Aiden shrugged Einarr's concern off. "Those words have been thrown at me nearly every day since I got here. Did you think hearing them from some strange chief would sting more than hearing it from our neighbors?"

"You should never have to hear such things at all." Einarr's face was lined with guilt, and Aiden pulled the other man closer to kiss those lines away.

"It's fine," he said, forcing a smile. "It's worth it for the time I get to spend with you."

"What happens, the day it isn't worth it?" Einarr asked, pain in his eyes. When Aiden only looked at him with confusion, he went on.

"It can't be enough, the little I give you, to make up for what you've lost. What you have to endure just living here. Learning an entirely new culture, leaving behind everyone you ever knew, the wounds of other people's ignorance... It isn't fair to you. I keep waiting for the day you realize it and demand to go home, or find someone else. For a moment, with Grímr I..."

Aiden stared at the other man, perplexed.

"Don't you realize I was thinking the same thing?" Aiden asked, baffled by how badly they'd misunderstood each other. "I expected every day to be the day you'd had enough of me. I kept trying to prepare myself for it, to keep from holding on too tightly in case you decided to throw me away. For a minute there with Grímr, I did consider leaving with him, because I thought it would be better than waiting for you to get tired of me. You could have anyone. Why would you ever choose me?"

"I would choose you over the gods themselves," Einarr said fiercely, fingers grazing Aiden's cheek and sliding into his hair. "If I lived my life a hundred times, I would always choose you. There's never been a person who loved me more totally than you. You've seen all my worst sides, and you still love me. The world is brighter with you in it, Aiden. How could I ever choose someone else?"

Tears stung Aiden's eyes, and he threw his arms around Einarr to hide them in the other man's chest. Einarr squeezed him close, pressing kisses to the top of Aiden's head.

"I forget sometimes," he said, "how new our relationship is, when it feels like I've loved you forever. I'll work harder at getting to know you, at understanding your feelings."

"I'll do better too," Aiden promised, "At trusting you, and telling you when things like this are bothering me."

"That's all I ask," Einarr said with a smile, leaning back to meet Aiden's eye. "I want to be with you forever. I love you, Aiden."

"I love you too, Einarr."

Aiden kissed the other man firmly, then wiped the tears from his eyes.

"Okay," he said when they were both stable again. "So, what do we do next?"

Chapter Fourteen

As Einarr had predicted, Grímr was kept alive and questioned by the chiefs. He told them his story without shame. Einarr sat in on the meetings, and Aiden listened from outside as Grímr spoke.

"I've been outlawed twenty years," he said, always calm and unafraid. "I had no family that would shelter me. I lived alone in the mountains above Ingifast, and I planned my revenge on Einarr, who I blamed for my condition. But I did not know where he had fled. Then, just earlier this season, I saw men of Ingifast kill Arrnjorn's sister, and I knew he would come seeking revenge, and bring Einarr with him. I waited outside Ingifast for the raid to begin, and then I ran into the fighting and found my enemy. When I saw him defending Aiden, I knew I could make him suffer better than just killing him. I took the boy and fled. I had planned to leave the country once my revenge was complete, and I had a boat hidden on the coast. As I ran, taking Aiden with me, we came across Bjorn's army. Einarr was close behind me, and I knew that, if I wanted to escape him, I would not have time to go around them. We slipped through in the night, and as we passed Bjorn's tent, we heard him arguing with his father. We watched through a gap in the tent as Hallvaror stabbed his father in the back."

"And why return?" one of the chiefs asked. "You know the penalty for breaking the conditions of your outlawry. Why not carry on and leave this country? Why present yourself to us? There are some here who think solitude has driven you mad, and you come to us looking for death."

"I came back because of Aiden," Grímr said plainly, and outside, Aiden's breath caught. "He earned my respect. He fought me, even injured and unarmed, every step of the way to get back to Einarr and Arnnstead. When it looked like we would both die in the wilderness, he could have let me starve, but chose to keep us both alive instead. Only when he thought this village was threatened did he ever beg. Only when he thought it was your lives in danger rather than his own did he plead with me to take him back. Aiden Broken-Shield is one of the most honorable men I've ever met. If his words are not enough to convince you, then nothing will be."

Aiden's heart ached to hear Grímr defending him that way, even after Aiden had refused him. Aiden wondered how painful it was for Grímr to be in this position again, laying down his life to defend someone he cared about from the law. It wasn't fair for him to be put through this twice. And Aiden certainly didn't intend for this to end with Grímr's death, after all they'd been through.

That night, Einarr stayed late in the hall, feasting with the chiefs who still deliberating, their decision set for the morning. Aiden went home alone and lay in bed, heart pounding in his ears, until Jódís and Agna had fallen asleep. Silently as he could, clutching his pine walking stick, he limped out of the house and through town to the empty shack where Grímr was being held. Once the chief's decision was made, he was to be put to death for breaking his outlawry. Aiden wasn't going to let that happen.

As he neared the shed, a bag of supplies over his shoulder, he heard voices coming from inside.

"Are you going to leave with me this time?" Grímr asked. "Like we planned all those years ago?"

"I should have left with you then."

Aiden's eyes widened, recognizing Einarr's voice, and he hesitated, listening.

"I was afraid," Einarr confessed. "I could make all the excuses in the world, but in the end, the truth is, I was afraid. I let you suffer alone because of that."

"I was afraid too," Grímr said quietly. "I'm still afraid. Your life was always too easy, Einarr. It made you kind, but it made you soft too. You were never made to choke down the fear like I was. But I wouldn't want to see the man that suffering would turn you in to. I shouldn't have asked you to come with me. I would have regretted it, seeing that kindness drain out of you."

"I suppose that makes Aiden better than both of us," Einarr said, shame in his voice. "He suffered, and he stayed kind."

"If you're only just realizing that," Grímr snorted, "You really don't deserve him."

"He really doesn't," Aiden added, slipping through the door with a smile. "Good thing I love him too much to care."

Grímr was tied to a beam in the center of the small building. Einarr knelt before him with a torch and supplies.

"Aiden, what are you—?" Einarr stammered as Aiden put his bag down.

"I had the same idea you did, I think," Aiden said with a shrug. "I came to help Grímr escape."

"I'm not escaping," Grímr denied them flatly, "With either of you. In the morning, if they see I'm gone, Aiden is the first person they'll turn on. I won't have him accused of treason for my sake."

"Then take him with you."

Aiden stared, briefly floored by Einarr's words.

"What are you talking about?" he asked, too confused to accept what he'd heard.

Einarr wouldn't meet his eye, brow furrowed with worry.

"I've been thinking about it since this afternoon," he said. "I love you. But loving you isn't enough to keep you safe. The people here are always going to hold what you used to be against you. And not just that, but what I made you as well. What I'm *still* making you. One day, I won't be there at the right time, like in Ingifast, and today in the hall, and you'll be..."

He trailed off, unable to finish the sentence, and looked at Grímr instead. Grímr looked back at him steadily.

"You would trust me with him?" Grímr asked. "After everything?"

"You were my best friend once," Einarr said with a wistful smile. "There was a time I loved you just as much as I love him now. Who else could I trust to keep him safe?"

169

"This is ridiculous," Aiden interrupted them. "Even if I did go along with this, they'd send men after us, which we can't afford with Hallvaror coming, and I'd still be blamed when they catch us."

"I'll take the blame," Einarr said calmly. "It's about time I got what was coming to me, anyway."

That stunned both of them silent for a moment.

"Don't be stupid," Grímr said at last, shrugging his shoulders against his bonds with an impatient huff. "The kid is never going to leave you, anyway. Trust me, I spent a week trying to keep him away from you. It's not going to work. Whatever issues you two have with the people here, you'll have to deal with them some other way."

Aiden looked away for a moment as they all considered what to do.

"All three of us could leave," Aiden suggested quietly, "Together."

"My family…" Einarr protested.

"Will miss you just as much if you die," Aiden finished for him. "We could bring them with us if you want. Or, at least Agna. I think Jódís has plans to remarry; she's been flirting with Gunnar lately."

"I couldn't force Agna to grow up an outlaw."

"But you could let her grow up an orphan?" Aiden pointed out the contradiction with a frown. "Besides, we don't have to stay here. We can leave the country, find somewhere new, and start again."

"Aiden…"

"It could work! Just give it a chance…"

"Or you could both just accept what I've been trying to tell you," Grímr said, stepping in between their argument. "That I'm not going to escape. No, listen to me."

Aiden started to protest, but Grímr cut him off, sighing with bitter exhaustion.

"I'm tired," he said. "Twenty years I've been running on nothing but anger, staying alive just so I could come back and kill the man I used to love. Now, I'm looking him in the face, and I can't even hate him. All I can remember is how it used to be. How it can never be again. And I'm tired. I just want it to be over. I don't mind dying. Dying for the sake of someone you love seems just as noble as dying in battle to me. So, just let it happen. And go live a happier life for me."

Aiden shook his head, anger and frustration making a tangled knot in his stomach. But he couldn't think of what to say. How to fix this awful situation they were trapped in.

"Aiden?" Einarr still wasn't looking at him, but staring at Grímr with a guilty expression on his face, "Can you forgive me for something I'm about to do?"

"Probably," Aiden replied, puzzled and unsure what to expect. Whatever ideas came to mind, what Einarr did was probably at the bottom of his list of likely possibilities.

Einarr leaned forward, caught Grímr by the back of his head, and kissed him hard. Aiden watched, stunned, as Grímr returned the kiss, crushing his mouth against Einarr's like he was starved for it.

Maybe he was. Aiden knew how long the man had been alone, how desperate he must be for this kind of attention. Where he'd expected jealousy to rise, he instead found himself pitying the love-starved outlaw and wishing he could help.

As Einarr pulled away, he tucked a knife back into his boot, and the bonds holding Grímr's hands fell away.

"You're not the only one who's been thinking about how things used to be," Einarr said, a little breathless. "Regardless of how things ended, of how things might end now, I never stopped caring about you, thinking about you. If this might be my last chance... I don't want you to spend the night alone."

He turned to Aiden then, stretching out a hand toward him, which Aiden took without thinking.

"I know you've never done anything like this before," Einarr's expression was a curious mix of guilt and hope, "But if you can..."

Aiden swallowed hard as Einarr pulled him closer, down to kneel between the two larger men. Einarr had told him that such relationships were normal and not frowned upon here. Faralder even had two wives. But Aiden had never seriously considered it a possibility. However, now, with Einarr's hands warm on his shoulders as he looked up into Grímr's still kiss-flushed face, Aiden wasn't sure he had the willpower to say no. Grímr was rubbing at his wrists, sore from the ropes, but as Einarr presented Aiden to him, he reached out at once, fingers hesitating an inch from

172

Aiden's cheek. There was a wild hope in his eyes, but wariness also, afraid of rejection.

"Is it alright?" he asked. "If you don't want to..."

"I want to," Aiden replied, making up his mind even as he spoke, catching Grímr's hand and pressing it to his cheek. "I want to."

He leaned closer, and Grímr's hand slid into his hair, pulling him closer into a bruising, desperate kiss, just as hungry and frantic as the one he'd shared with Einarr. Aiden felt Einarr lean over him, his chest pressed to Aiden's back as he dropped kisses over Grímr's neck and collar. Together, Aiden and Einarr showered Grímr in the affection he'd been denied so many years.

Grímr pulled Aiden closer, into his lap, his tongue hot and demanding as it pushed into Aiden's mouth. Einarr was tugging at Grímr's tunic, disrupting their kiss briefly to rid the outlaw of it. He pressed close to Grímr's left side, Aiden on the right, and his hands and mouth wandered freely, stroking and teasing. Aiden could tell from the little moans and shudders muffled by their kiss that Einarr still remembered the places that made Grímr weak.

Grímr's hands were at Aiden's hips, but hesitated to touch anywhere else. Aiden, impatient, lifted his shirt with one hand and pulled Grímr's palm to his stomach with the other. Grímr, seemingly reassured, stopped holding back, his fingers exploring every inch of Aiden he could reach, making Aiden jump and gasp when his surprisingly gentle touches found a sensitive spot. He seemed particularly

173

fascinated with the muscles of Aiden's back, running both hands up Aiden's shirt to trail fingers over his shoulder blades and down the ridges of his spine in a way that made Aiden's breath catch.

Grímr broke the kiss with a gasp and, dazed, Aiden looked over to see Einarr palming Grímr through his pants.

"Didn't want you to forget I was here," Einarr chuckled, and Aiden leaned over to kiss the other man, wondering if he could taste Grímr on his lips. As Aiden was focused on Einarr, Grímr began to undress him, tugging Aiden's tunic off over his head and beginning to pull down his leggings, stopping before his injured leg. Aiden shivered as the cool air hit his skin, followed by Grímr's heated hands, squeezing his hips and pulling him down to grind against his lap. Einarr's lips and teeth devoured Aiden's throat, leaving marks of ownership wet on his skin while Grímr scattered kisses over his back and shoulders. The two men met over Aiden's collarbone and kissed passionately, Einarr's hands teasing Aiden's chest as the smaller man's hips rocked against Grímr's lap.

Aiden had thought making love to Einarr was overwhelming before. This was dizzying. He could barely keep track of whose hands were on him, which lips he was kissing at any given moment. He only knew that there was nowhere he'd rather be. He wanted to show Grímr so much love that the man found his will to live again. They would figure out a way they could all live and be together. Now that Aiden knew what it felt like to have Einarr's oil-slicked fingers sliding into him while Grímr's rough, tender hands stroked his hardening shaft, he never wanted to give this up.

He turned to face Grímr and the bulge in the man's pants which he'd been teasing, pulling his breeches down to finally get a look at it. It was thicker than Einarr's, and almost as long, half-hard and deliciously heavy in Aiden's hand. Careful of his leg, he knelt and bent his head to taste it, feeling self-conscious at the way Grímr stared down at him with a kind of desperate, trembling hunger. Einarr's hands forced Aiden's hips higher for a better view as he stretched and prepared the younger man, taking his time to do it carefully. Aiden was equally thorough and methodical with slowly teasing Grímr to full hardness. He wet the surface liberally with his tongue first, noting that though Grímr's skin was darker than Einarr's, it was no less soft here, like silk around a steel column. Grímr's hand shook as he ran his fingers through Aiden's hair, and Aiden could tell he was fighting the urge to pull it, to drag Aiden's teasing lips down on to him properly. Aiden felt an unexpected thrill at the thought of such roughness, and wondered if he could tease the cautious outlaw into actually trying it. He stroked the shaft as his lips moved over the head, occasionally losing focus with a needy whimper as Einarr's fingers brushed against a sweet spot within him. He squirmed, trying to hold back his own pleasure and focus on Grímr, whose head he'd only barely engulfed when Einarr reached around to stroke him, laughing at how hard and dripping he found the smaller man.

"Don't!" Aiden gasped, pulling off of Grímr as he fought back pleasure, "Not yet!"

"Don't worry," Einarr chuckled, giving Aiden a teasing squeeze. "We have all night."

"But—"

Aiden could manage no more, all but drooling into Grímr's lap as Einarr stroked and fingered him at the same time. Grímr caught Aiden's chin and guided the younger man back to his dick, while Aiden struggled to focus on past the pleasure Einarr was giving him.

"You're too stubborn," Einarr chuckled as Aiden continued to hold out, pressing hard on Aiden's prostate and stroking him quickly at the same time. Aiden moaned around Grímr's dick, and the outlaw's willpower seemed to break. His grip on Aiden's hair tightened, and he pulled Aiden closer, forcing himself deeper into Aiden's throat. Aiden coughed and sputtered, caught by surprise, but as Grímr pulled him back, looking apologetic, Aiden was grinning, licking his lips in a daze. He felt light-headed, his head hammering, but he'd liked it.

He shifted with the help of the other two men until he was in Grímr's lap, his back to the outlaw's chest and his legs over Einarr's shoulders. He bit his lip as the two of them carefully lowered Aiden onto Grímr's tool, shivering as he felt the first heat of it, pressing into him and stretching him open. He wrapped his arms around Einarr's shoulders, trembling, his dick aching, as Grímr slowly slid into him. He'd never been with anyone else but Einarr before. So this was what another man's tool felt like inside him. It was so different— not just the thickness, but the shape, the curve. It felt totally new within him. He whimpered Grímr's name into Einarr's ear and felt the blond man squeeze him tighter in response.

He felt his backside connect with Grímr's hips sharply as the other man bottomed out inside him, the sensation of his dick, thick and full and pulsing inside him, pushing Aiden over the edge. He trembled and squeezed tighter as he came, panting a string of curses that made both men laugh.

"I wasn't even touching you," Einarr purred, kissing Aiden's throat. "I remember him being good, but not that good."

"It's... your fault... for winding me up like that!" Aiden gasped, flustered, still trying to come down from the orgasm and unable to completely settle when every tiny shift made the other man move inside him again.

"Don't fall apart on us yet." Grímr's voice was a lust-filled rumble in his ear, rough with desire. "If I'm going to the underworld tomorrow, I intend to enjoy tonight to the fullest."

If Aiden's head wasn't still spinning, he would have shuddered with eager anticipation at those words. Grímr began to move inside him, short, shallow thrusts up into him, encouraging him to move his hips himself. Aiden, still only beginning to recover, obliged as Einarr shifted just a little closer, taking

Aiden's hands from his shoulders and bringing them to his own aching need. Aiden wrapped both hands around the other man and stroked him in time to the movement of his hips, loving the way both men responded to his attention. He kissed Einarr again, then Grímr, leaning back against the outlaw's chest for support as he bucked in his lap, supported and guided by Grímr's rough hands. Once he was hard again, which didn't take long, Einarr pressed the length of his shaft against Aiden's, the motion of Grímr's thrusts grinding Aiden's tool against Einarr's. Aiden struggled to contain his voice, the feeling of both of them teasing him at the same time this way almost too much to bear. He wanted more.

"Please," he gasped, rolling his hips down to take Grímr deeper, "Harder."

Grímr met Einarr's eye over Aiden's shoulder, and they moved Aiden onto his knees again, tucking their clothes under Aiden's bad leg to cushion it. Einarr pulled Aiden's head down toward his stiff need without a hint of shyness. Grímr pulled Aiden's hips up to a height he liked, sliding his dick between the younger man's oil-slicked cheeks for a moment before he pressed in again, Aiden's hole opening easily for him now. He slid in all at once, hips striking Aiden's backside with a slap that made Aiden yelp and see stars.

"Is that what you were after?" Grímr asked. Aiden could only moan his reply, his mouth still full of Einarr. Perhaps hoping for a better answer, Grímr pulled back and slammed in again, making Aiden shake with pleasure as the impact raced through him. He set up a quick, rough rhythm, almost feral in the way he clung to Aiden, breeding him like an animal in heat. Every thrust forced Aiden further onto Einarr's dick, pushing it deeper into his throat in a way that made Aiden short of breath and obscenely excited. He didn't know why this rough treatment felt so good, but he loved it. Maybe it was just because it was coming from two men he trusted, who he knew would never want to cause him any real harm. He could relax and let them do whatever they wanted to him and he'd never have to be afraid. And the idea of letting the two of them have their way with him like that was enough to bring Aiden close to cumming again.

Grímr beat him to it, speeding up his pace suddenly at the same time Einarr caught the back of Aiden's head and forced him deeper than ever, holding him in place there while Grímr thrust in as deeply as he could on the other side, to leave his mark as deeply within Aiden as he could, somewhere it could never be washed out. Einarr finished a moment later, pouring his seed directly down Aiden's throat. Aiden pulled away, coughing and choking and wiping reflexive tears from his eyes, only for Grímr to suddenly pull him close and lick the remaining cum from his lips and cheeks. Aiden blushed, thrilled and scandalized. He kissed Aiden deeply, his beard scratching Aiden's over sensitive skin, as Einarr moved between Aiden's legs to return the favor, the heat of his mouth quickly bringing Aiden to a second, bone-shaking release.

He slumped against Grímr's chest, shaking with pleasure and exhaustion. Einarr soon came to warm his other side, and Grímr put an arm around both of them. They sat, tangled in each other, breathing heavily, drunk on passion and intimacy, until they'd recovered enough for the lust to take them again.

Eventually, spent, they lay on the floor of the shack with their arms around each other, Grímr in the center, and Aiden allowed himself to drift off, listening to the quiet murmurs of the other two talking above him.

"Do you remember that first time, on the moor?"

"There were blue bells everywhere, and little white dryas flowers in your hair."

"I thought I'd never love someone that much again."

"Neither did I..."

Aiden slept hard, and woke as someone was picking him up.

"What's going on?" he muttered, rubbing his eyes.

"Just moving you to the bed," Einarr said softly. "Go back to sleep."

Aiden closed his eyes again without complaint, and Einarr kissed his cheek.

"I love you, Aiden. So much."

He woke again when the horse beneath him stumbled on a stone, jerking to alertness as he realized the motion he'd been dismissing as Einarr carrying him had a long while ago transitioned into the smooth gait of Grímr's horse. He was sitting in front of the outlaw, curled against his chest.

"What's going on?" Aiden asked, panic fluttering in his chest like a startled bird. "Where are we?"

The sky was still a soft dove gray, the sun not yet fully risen. Mist like ragged white silk drifted around the horse's hooves and cascaded down the green hills from the stony slate of the mountains above them. On Aiden's left, the ocean rushed with the incoming tide, wearing down the stony beaches. Grímr kept a tight grip on Aiden to keep the younger man's frantic twisting from throwing him off the horse.

"We're outside of Arnnstead," Grímr explained. "Escaping."

"Where's Einarr?" was Aiden's next question, though he had a horrible sense that he already knew.

"He stayed behind," Grímr said, confirming Aiden's fears.

"We have to go back!" Aiden cried at once, turning to try and look back the way he'd come, like against all logic, Einarr would be there riding after them. "We have to turn around right now! We can't let him do this!"

"He wanted this." Grímr caught Aiden by the shoulder and shook him, shocking him out of his panic, "He thinks he has to. To make up for what happened to me."

"But he's *wrong*." Aiden felt terrified tears welling in his eyes at the thought of Einarr being held for execution. "We have to talk sense into him before it's too late! We can think of a different plan!"

"It's already too late," Grímr replied, stubbornly trying not to look at Aiden's pleading expression. "This is the plan he's chosen. Now, calm down. Calm down!"

Aiden was struggling now, fighting to get off the horse, and Grímr had to pull the beast to a stop before Aiden hurt himself, holding the smaller man in place.

"They aren't going to kill him!" Grímr shouted. "Would you relax and listen to me? Einarr is Arnnjorn's heir. They won't execute him lightly, especially not when they have much bigger things to worry about right now. They'll hold him for sentencing later."

"So we are going to rescue him?" Aiden asked, confused.

"No," Grímr replied, "We're going to use this opportunity to cripple Hallvaror's army. Hopefully, when they see what we've done, there will be no need to rescue Einarr."

Aiden punched Grímr in the arm, and the man flinched, blinking at him in confusion.

"What was that for?"

"You could have woken me up and explained the plan to me!" Aiden snapped. "How would you feel just waking up on a horse, leaving the people you love behind?"

He swore, hit Grímr again, and then turned around to face forward, determined to stubbornly ignore the other man for a few hours at least. Grímr, without another word, got the horse moving again, heading up the coast. Aiden's plan for chilly silence didn't last long, as he realized he still didn't know where they were going.

"So, what is the plan?" he asked, not looking back. "How are we stopping Hallvaror?"

"Even if the chiefs join together against Hallvaror, their army won't be big enough to stop him. We have to slow him down long enough for someone who can stop him to arrive..."

Chapter Fifteen

What happened next happened fast. When Aiden and Grímr left Arnnstead, Hallvaror's army was likely to reach the first coastal villages in only a few days. The chiefs, expecting this, were ready, and baffled when, three days later, there was no sign of the approaching army. Scouts reported it was still several days out, and smaller now than previously reported. Word reached Arnnstead that, as expected, Hallvaror had refused the call to ting, and now the other jarls were sending men to fetch him by force all the way back to Uppsala to face judgement before the temple of the gods. If word of this had reached them in Arnnstead, surely Hallvaror's army had heard it as well. Perhaps that was the cause for their delay and decreased size?

And then, further confusing matters, scouts reported a second army on the move, at least the equal of Hallvaror's, heading down the coast toward them. Arnnjorn stood on the hill above his village, looking out at the two armies he could now see approaching, and wondered what would become of him and his home.

And then, as the second army drew closer, the scouts reported a man with hair the color of fire was leading it, riding alongside Jarl Eiláfr of Sigtuna.

Aiden rode, head high, next to the mighty jarl, hoping that, though he knew it was unlikely, Einarr could see him right now wherever he was. The baffled staring of the villagers as Aiden approached was more than a little satisfying as well.

"Aiden!" Arnnjorn called out a greeting as Aiden and the Jarl left their men at the edge of town and rode toward the hall. "I wondered where you had disappeared to. I half suspected that outlaw had run off with you again. And Jarl Eiláfr! It's an honor to meet such a man of legend."

"I wish I was here on more cheerful business, Arnnjorn Egilson." Jarl Eiláfr, a massive man with a dark, thorny beard, seemed to look at no one but the horizon when he spoke, his voice a rumble like thunder in the distance. "But I am here on a matter of justice. Uppsala called for Hallvaror Bjornson and he refused the call. This would be crime enough, even should the charges of cowardice against him prove false. I could not let such a man go to war, and risk the warriors he met in battle being refused entry to Valhalla for being felled by a coward. Your messenger here made the urgency of the matter clear, and I agree. The gods cannot be kept waiting."

"Oh, don't worry," Arnnjorn laughed, "I intend to introduce that little golden shit to the gods myself."

Jarl Eiláfr smiled, which was the closest Aiden had seen the man come to genuine emotion since they'd met.

"And you..." Arnnjorn turned to Aiden. "Now is not the time, but if you live through the battle to come, you and Einarr will have much to answer for."

"So, he is still alive?" Aiden asked, relief flooding him.

"Of course," Arnnjorn scoffed. "This would be a foolish time to be executing one of my best warriors. He's been refusing to speak. I take it this was why he set the outlaw loose?"

"Can I see him?" Aiden asked, not answering the question.

"Do you plan to run off with him?"

"Not this time."

"Then he's in the same shed we had the outlaw in. Make it quick. We don't have much time now."

Aiden turned his horse in that direction at once as Arnnjorn took Jarl Eiláfr to discuss the upcoming battle with the other chiefs.

"Aiden!"

Einarr stared in shock as Aiden burst through the door of his prison. Aiden wasted no time in dropping his walking stick and throwing himself across the little room to where Einarr sat tied to a beam. He hugged the other man tightly, showering his face with kisses.

"What are you doing here?" Einarr asked, confused and worried. "You're supposed to be far away from here, somewhere safe!"

"Yes, while you died to make up for something that happened twenty years ago." Aiden rolled his eyes, untying Einarr's arms so that the other man could hold him. "That was a stupid plan. Grímr and I came up with a better one."

"Which involved what, exactly?" Einarr was eyeing Aiden more closely now, taking in the fine new leather armor he was wearing and the new axe at his waist.

"First, we rode toward Hallvaror's army," Aiden explained, "And spent a few days hobbling them in any way we could. Spilling their water, spoiling their food, releasing their animals, setting fire to their tents. No one is better at moving quickly and silently through those hills than Grímr. As soon as they were slowed, men started leaving, already suspicious of Bjorn's death and further convinced the gods had turned against them thanks to the sabotage. We knew once that happened that it was safe to leave and ride for Sigtuna. I remembered your stories about the other jarls of this country, and how devout Jarl Eiláfr was. I knew he'd never tolerate Hallvaror's refusal to respect tradition. Grímr brought me to meet the Jarl and help me convince him, then rode back to continue harrying Hallvaror's forces until Eiláfr's armies could reach Arnnstead. Between Eiláfr's men and the chiefs that have joined us, I think we might actually have Hallvaror outnumbered."

Such underhanded tactics were usually seen as sneaky and unmanly by the Northmen, but for Aiden and Grímr, an argr thrall and an outlaw, it could hardly damage their reputation any further.

"How?" Einarr stammered, delight overtaking his confusion. "Aiden, you're a miracle! A gift from the gods!"

He grabbed Aiden and kissed him hard, clearly overjoyed.

"Where is Grímr now?" he asked when they parted. "Is he safe?"

"He's still keeping an eye on Hallvaror," Aiden explained, "But he'll be back before the battle starts. Which won't be long. All Arnnjorn's men are ready, and Hallvaror is coming."

"Luck seems to be on our side today," Einarr laughed. "Maybe he'll see Jarl Eiláfr's army and run away!"

"Are you two done cuddling yet?"

Faralder stuck his head through the door, Branulf lurking behind him.

"We've come to bring our esteemed prisoner his weapon."

He presented Einarr's sword with a flourish.

"Arnnjorn intends to let me fight?" Einarr asked. "Isn't he worried I'll run?"

"We all know you better than that, Einarr," Branulf said. "And we need our best today. So, get ready. The enemy is almost upon us."

"We have something for you too, Broken-Shield," Faralder said with a grin, taking a shield from Branulf and handing it to Aiden. He recognized it after a moment as the split round shield he'd used in the raid on Ingifast, it's break filled in with metal like a jagged silver lightning bolt through the center of the circle.

"This shield seemed to be good luck for you last time," Faralder said. "I mean, apart from the whole kidnapping thing. It seemed like you should have it back."

188

Aiden strapped it to his arm with a grin.

"Thank you, Faralder. And you, Branulf."

Faralder beamed, but Branulf looked away, huffing like it meant nothing. Aiden had always thought Branulf didn't like him much, or rather didn't like the threat Aiden was to Einarr's reputation. But he knew Faralder hadn't done this metal work. That was Branulf's specialty. Aiden smiled, pleased to have finally earned the other man's approval.

"Alright," Einarr said, handing Aiden back his abandoned walking stick and taking his sword from Faralder. "Let's go and see what the gods have planned for us."

Chapter Sixteen

The joined armies of the chiefs of the coastal villages were gathering outside Arnnstead, on the hills above the town. Jarl Eiláfr's men had come up from the beach to join them there as well. Just as they had last winter, Jarl Bjorn's army, now Jarl Hallvaror's, was coming over the hills toward Arnnstead, albeit much more raggedly now. They must have passed through several other towns on their way here and found them empty and known there was an army gathered here to wait for them, but they could not have anticipated the size of the force waiting for them.

Aiden was near the front with Einarr, Faralder, and Branulf. The chiefs were all in sight, each with their own force, making last minute plans and strategies for how the disparate armies would work together. Aiden wasn't far from Arnnjorn, and he saw Grímr the moment the outlaw rode up to the chief to deliver his news.

"Most of them know of the accusations against Hallvaror now," he reported. "Those that are still with him either stay out of misplaced loyalty to Bjorn, or genuine loyalty to Hallvaror. A good few of them say he was right to kill Bjorn. The good news is most of them don't have shoes anymore."

He dumped a sack full of boots at Arnnjorn's feet, who roared with laughter.

"If I'd had you with us last winter," Arnnjorn chuckled, wiping his eyes, "I doubt there'd be anything left of that army by now. I don't normally approve of trickery, but I won't refuse the gift. Thank you."

Grímr bowed his head in acceptance of the gratitude and swung off his horse, offering its reins to Arnnjorn, his eyes already on Aiden and Einarr.

"Also, I believe this was yours."

Arnnjorn looked mildly confused for a moment, until he recognized his sword hanging from the horse's side and realized it was the same horse and the same sword Grímr had taken from him at Ingifast. He looked outraged at first, then laughed, shaking his head. Grímr was already moving past him to embrace Aiden and Einarr.

"It's good to see you alive," Grímr said as Einarr held him close. "I was worried for a moment that we might have overestimated Arnnjorn's good sense."

"I doubt he would have had me killed even if he'd had time to judge me for releasing you," Einarr reassured the other man, clapping him on the back. "He didn't even care that much about executing you."

"You always were too damn lucky," Grímr grumbled, but Aiden could tell the man was relieved.

A horn blew, alerting them to the enemy army's approach.

"Guess he isn't going to run after all," Aiden said, swinging on to the horse that Jarl Eiláfr had loaned him. "Shame."

"Both of you stay close to me," Einarr ordered. "Either all three of us meet in Asgard tonight, or none of us do."

"The only man I could ever accept killing me is standing next to me," Grímr declared, beating his axe against his chest and shaking his arms as he worked himself up. "If I died at any other hand, I would crawl back out of the underworld myself to correct it."

"I feel the same," Einarr said with a grin.

"Then you should both live a very long time," Aiden added, looking a little pale. "In which case, you should be keeping an eye on me. In case you've forgotten, my leg is still broken."

In case he lost his horse, he had his walking stick tied to his shield arm so that he could defend himself while keeping the weight off of his leg, and Yrsa the healer had given him enough of the pain killing 'warrior's herb' that he could hardly feel his leg at all except for a vague tingling where his toes were.

"You really probably should have stayed in town," Einarr agreed, worried for a moment.

"With the women and elderly?" Aiden scoffed, offended. "I'm still a man! And a man doesn't turn his back on a fight when the people he loves are at risk. Even if his leg is broken."

"I already tried talking him out of it," Grímr told Einarr tiredly. "Just give up now. I've never met someone so stubborn. If I get killed because I was worrying about you and your leg—"

"I thought you couldn't be killed by anyone but Einarr?"

"I really think you should both be focusing on—"

A second horn blew. The enemy was charging. Jarl Eiláfr gave a bellow and raced forward, his men spilling after him, and the other chiefs followed suit. Grímr moved first, roaring like a great beast as he ran, and Aiden and Einarr rushed after him, Aiden on his horse, readying a spear.

The two armies collided like crashing waves, and death followed immediately. Aiden jabbed downwards with his spear at the men on the ground, focusing on defending his horse primarily, and also trampling any man that raised a weapon toward Einarr or Grímr. He hardly needed to worry about Grímr. It seemed living as an outlaw had only improved Grímr's fighting abilities. He fought like a wild animal, raging teeth and claw at his enemies, unfazed by any injury.

"How does he do that?" Aiden asked, his horse rearing to swing its hooves at an enemy, distracting the man while Einarr put a sword through him.

"He didn't tell you?" Einarr laughed victoriously as he pulled his sword free and swung it again. "Grímr is a berserker!"

The three men stayed close as they waded deeper into the fray. Grímr was savagely powerful, but easily overwhelmed by too many enemies. Einarr guarded the outlaw's back while Aiden picked off any other threats from his horse.

He swore as, catching him off guard, someone appeared practically beneath his horses hooves, frightening it. It reared back and, unprepared, Aiden tumbled off with a shout. Grímr was there in a second, keeping the enemy preoccupied while Einarr got Aiden to his feet, but from then on, slowed by Aiden's leg, they could no longer move freely. They struggled to keep up with the rest of the men, finding themselves more and more often surrounded by the enemy. Aiden could see Einarr beginning to wear down, and though Grímr's berserker rage showed no sign of slowing, Aiden knew he couldn't keep it up forever.

"Einarr, this way!"

Aiden, hiding behind his shield and jabbing at an enemy with his axe ineffectually, looked up to see Faralder and Branulf, both injured but still fighting, clearing a path.

Aiden dropped his shield long enough to hook his opponent's shoulder with the beard of his axe, dragging the man close enough to bash his nose in on the metal of Aiden's shield. Then he retreated quickly to Einarr's side. Einarr had a grip on Grímr's tunic, yanking the nearly senseless man back toward the safety Faralder and Branulf were offering.

Back among their own men, no longer so immersed in the fray, Aiden began to realize how exhausted and in pain he was— things he'd been ignoring for the sake of surviving. Despite the fact that he felt like he'd been kicked by a herd of horses, from here, it was easy to see they were winning, forcing Hallvaror's army back over the hills and into a valley that would easily be their death if they were foolish enough to stay there.

"What's happening?" Einarr asked Faralder as they took a moment to catch their breath, safe for the moment with so many of their own warriors around them.

"Jarl Eiláfr intends to fall back once he has Hallvaror pinned in that valley," Branulf explained, "To give Hallvaror's men a chance to change sides. He wants as few as possible to die in service of a coward."

"He's a bit loony if you ask me." Faralder, drenched in blood and slightly terrifying, grinned like a madman. "Devotion to the gods is good and all, but if those men haven't backed out by now, their honor won't let them."

"I just can't believe we're winning." Aiden leaned against Einarr's side, panting and exhausted, his walking stick broken off. "I was still really certain we were going to lose."

"As Eiláfr would say," Faralder laughed, "The gods are on our side today. But I think you should go and lay down, little friend. Passing out on the battlefield and getting trampled would be a terribly embarrassing way to go."

Aiden considered arguing, but the medicine Yrsa had given him was wearing off, and it was getting hard to think about anything except how much his leg hurt.

"Alright," he mumbled, giving in. "Laying down sounds good."

"He agreed?" Grímr muttered, only just beginning to come out of his rage. "He really must be hurt."

Yrsa had a tent safely behind their lines where she was tending the injured. Grímr and Einarr got

Aiden there and saw him safely laid down before returning to the fight.

"Don't do anything too dangerous without me," Aiden demanded, words slurred with exhaustion and the medicine Yrsa had thrown at him. "I mean it."

"We wouldn't dare die without you there," Einarr said with a laugh, and kissed Aiden's forehead before he left, unconcerned about who saw. Grímr, more reserved, brought Aiden's hand to his lips instead.

"Rest," he ordered. "The fighting won't go on much longer today."

Then they were both gone, and Aiden was sinking into exhausted sleep.

The Northmen had a way of making all but the most hellish parts of battle seem glorious. Aiden had loved fighting beside Grímr and Einarr. The killing was awful, blood stinking and greasy on his skin. He hated the fear and the press of bodies. But somehow, being there, next to the other two men made it not just worth it, but exhilarating. He felt like he could have fought beside them forever. Three warriors, seeking glory and victory...

In his dreams, it was not so. He was lost in the clash of men and weapons, and Einarr and Grímr were nowhere in sight, except when he discovered their bodies, which he did over and over, finding them slaughtered in increasingly awful ways each time. Fighting next to them was like something out of a story, but there was only one way such a story could end. The thought made Aiden nauseous, and he woke retching. It was late, the tent pitch dark but for a low-lit lamp hanging from the room far at the other end, where Yrsa and the other healers were still at work, talking quietly as they sewed shut a wound.

Aiden sat up slowly, and in the dim light, realized Einarr and Grímr both were both close by, sitting against the wall near him, leaning against one another as they slept. Grímr's many wounds, some superficial, others more dangerous, had been tended. Einarr's eye had been rebandaged. The tent, and no doubt others like it, was packed to capacity with injured men. Some, Aiden knew, wouldn't live to see the morning. Likely, many were already dead. He scanned the injured for familiar faces, wondering if anyone he knew was among the dead or dying. Even in a fight they were winning, there would still be losses. This was accepted, even celebrated, among the Norse. No warrior was afraid of dying in battle. But Aiden couldn't help doubting, fearing. The halls of the honored dead might be packed with righteous souls, but Aiden would still rather have them here, alive, and in the case of two, sleeping beside him. He rolled over, the better to reach out to the sleeping men. Grímr was closer, his sleeping face scrunched in some nightmare. Aiden stroked his cheek and took his hand, watching the fear melt from his roughhewn features. As long as they stayed together, Aiden told himself as he drifted back to sleep, Valhalla would never have them, and that was how Aiden preferred it.

Chapter Seventeen

He woke to the sound of a horn, crying from their defensive line at the first light of dawn. Men were approaching the camp. Einarr had found Aiden a new walking stick— the broken end of a spear— and Aiden scrambled for it as he stumbled tiredly out of the healer's tent. Einarr staggered out after him. Grímr, ever vigilant, was already awake.

"It looks like Faralder was wrong," the outlaw said. "Jarl Eiláfr's offer must have got through to some of them. Must be half of his remaining forces. He's not going to be happy when he sees them gone."

Jarl Eiláfr and a few of the other chiefs were greeting Hallvaror's deserters, taking their weapons and having them led to a holding area for prisoners. They'd be released when the fighting was over, but no one could risk them changing their minds about which side they were on during the fighting. But as the deserters moved past the Jarl, one of them moved suddenly, darting closer to Eiláfr. Thin and dirty, Aiden would not have recognized him if not for his wild blond hair. Hallvaror Bjornson pulled a knife from his clothes and drove it under Jarl Eiláfr's chin. At once, the men around him revealed weapons as well, throwing themselves at the unprepared warriors.

"Idiots!" Hallvaror screamed like a madman, waving his sword so wildly he endangered his own men. "Cowards! If you had joined me, the empire of the Norse could have lived forever! Now, England will bury your children! But you will not live to see it!"

Aiden, realizing they were outnumbered and underprepared, grabbed Einarr and Grímr both and yanked them backwards away from the fighting. After a moment of confusion, they followed, Einarr scooping Aiden up so they could move faster. As they did, they saw the other half of Hallvaror's army coming at them from the other side. They must have circled around in the night. They were still vastly outnumbered, but surprise would see a lot of men killed. Horns were blowing frantically, alerting the entire army that they were under attack. Einarr, Aiden, and Grímr ducked back into the medical tent to regroup.

"We have to take out Hallvaror," Aiden said, already tightening the brace on his leg and reaching for his shield. "The others may stop fighting if they see him defeated."

"We'll never get past the men around him," Einarr protested.

"Yes, you will." Yrsa shocked all three of them, the old healer woman appearing behind them like a ghost. "And most importantly, you won't let them get near this tent."

She slammed a small barrel she was holding down on the floor.

"Pitch," she explained, "For torches and wounds."

Aiden's eyes lit up, seeing where she was going with this.

"How many do you have?"

A minute later, the chaos of the surprise attack exploded into fire as Yrsa's pitch barrels, now on fire, rolled into the heart of Hallvaror's men and right to the young Jarl's feet. His men shouted and threw themselves clear of the fire, and Einarr, Aiden, and Grímr were there to take advantage, leaping through the opening they'd made. It was Einarr who took Hallvaror on, sword against sword, as Grímr swung his axe at anyone who got too close, and Aiden, limping along with barrel of pitch on his back and a torch in his hand, hurled flaming rags covered in hot tar at whoever dared look in his direction. When the surprise of that ceased to be effective, he dropped the barrel and took out his axe, guarding with his shield as he glanced back to see how Einarr was doing.

The warrior seemed to be in a standoff with the mad jarl, the two circling each other, Einarr easily blocking, but unable to properly attack past Hallvaror's crazed, maniac thrashing. Had losing driven him so crazy? Or had he already been on his way toward madness when he murdered his father?

His view of Einarr was abruptly cut off by another warrior, swinging at him with a huge axe. Aiden usually relied on being nimble when faced with a larger, stronger opponent, but with his leg in this condition, that was less of an option. He relied on being unexpected instead, throwing himself down and sinking his hand axe into the man's ankle, rolling out of the way of his enemy's axe and then his body as it came crashing down. He was on his knees a second later, and his axe found the man's throat, finishing the job.

He struggled onto his feet just in time to catch another blow on his shield, and he looked around for Grímr frantically, needing help to stand back up. He felt his heart skip a beat as he realized he couldn't see the man. He couldn't find Einarr, either. They were meant to stay together...

He threw off the spear stuck in his shield and hurried through the mess of fighting men, forced to stop and defend himself with almost every step. When he was fighting, he could focus on nothing but that or risk death. But every other second, his eyes were searching faces frantically. He remembered his nightmare of the evening before and felt his gut churn with fear at the thought of finding the faces he was searching for lying in the dirt, eyes clouded with blood.

A familiar face loomed out of the melee at last, but not the one he'd hoped for. Hallvaror, injured but alive, his eyes wild, threw himself against Aiden's shield, stabbing past it with his sword. Aiden only just managed to avoid the wild stabs, throwing the Jarl off.

"You!" Hallvaror howled. "I remember you! Thrall! Nothing! You were the sneak thief outside my tent that night! You've cost us everything!"

He lunged at Aiden single-mindedly, a surprising amount of skill behind his mad swings, and Aiden could only defend himself, terrified. He couldn't even swing back at the other man, hesitating every time he thought he saw an opening. Hallvaror, a Jarl's son, had likely been trained by skilled masters. Aiden had only begun learning to fight since he'd come to live here. But most importantly, he simply couldn't think about Hallvaror right now. Where were Einarr and Grímr?

He spotted Grímr first, that raging beast, grown alone in the cold mountains, a feral wolf crouched over a body, gutting anyone in reach with axe and knife, his eyes alive with bloodlust. But he was injured, weakening, the enemy outnumbering him, getting in strikes more and more, which slowly sapped the berserker's energy. And then, Aiden realized the body he was crouching over was not a fallen foe, but Einarr, his wheat-colored hair tumbled in the mud and his eyes unseeing. Terror flashed through Aiden like lightning, setting his nerve endings on fire. He needed to get to Einarr. Nothing mattered but getting to Einarr, and right now, Hallvaror was in his way.

It was as though his injured leg didn't exist anymore. He couldn't feel the pain, couldn't feel anything but the all-consuming fear for his lover's life. Hallvaror was fighting without a shield, too crazed to care about defense. Aiden charged him, screaming, and caught the wild blow of the mad Jarl's sword on his shield. He felt the blade bite deep, past the shield and into his shoulder, but he ignored it, driving forward instead to bash Hallvaror under the chin. The Jarl stumbled backwards, pulling his sword free, and Aiden went after him, not giving him time to recover. A wild swing of Hallvaror's sword connected with Aiden's arm, and he thanked whatever gods were watching that he'd caught the flat, not the blade, but the shock opened his hand and he dropped his axe, lost in the mud and battle. Aiden threw himself at the Jarl anyway, guarding his left side with his shield as he collided with Hallvaror's chest, driving him to the ground, knocking the wind from him. In the brief moment he was stunned, Aiden bashed the hard metal edge of the shield into the man's sword hand hard enough to break his fingers, forcing him to drop the sword. Hallvaror howled with rage and threw Aiden over, heavier and stronger, pinning Aiden to the mud with his hands around the smaller man's throat.

"This was supposed to be my legacy!" Hallvaror howled. "I was meant to be a god!"

Aiden scrabbled at the fingers crushing his windpipe as his vision went dark, straining for some way, any way, to escape this.

Something, someone, collided with Hallvaror, driving the breath from him with an audible grunt. Aiden struggled to recover as Branulf rolled to his feet, the stout man heavily injured, but still as formidable as ever. The Jarl stumbled, but caught his bearings and lunged at Branulf, only to be intercepted by Faralder, covered in blood like war paint and whooping like a madman as he battered Hallvaror with the staff of a broken spear, the only weapon he or Branulf had left. Hallvaror screamed his rage and tried to tackle Faralder, tear him apart with his bare hands, but the skinny warrior was always dancing just out of his reach to crack him over the head with his stick again until Hallvaror was dazed and stumbling and even more furious than before. Then, Faralder stepped out of the way.

Arnnjorn Eagle-Bear came charging out of the fray like a demon out of hell, huge and furious, and he'd buried his sword in Hallvaror's gut before the Jarl had a chance to react— buried it with such force, it lifted the man off his feet and into the air. Aiden watched in awe, knowing he was seeing something that would be written in the sagas for generations. No one there, including Hallvaror's men, could help but stop and stare at the sight of Arnnjorn, huge and ferocious, hoisting the mad jarl into the air, backlit by the rising sun, his wild hair a golden halo. The moment seemed to go on forever.

Then Arnnjorn threw Hallvaror down, all but flinging the man off of his sword.

"It is done!" he bellowed. "Hallvaror Bjornson is dead! The gods have turned against him and proven his cowardice! Throw down your weapons now and return to your families as living fools rather than shameful corpses!"

As Aiden watched, the men around them began to lower their weapons, disgrace in their eyes. They knew to die now would bring them no glory. Some would fight anyway, but Aiden could see the wave of defeat spreading, the battle stilling. He didn't care. His eyes searched the crowd for the only two faces that mattered.

Arnnjorn was shouting his victory still, the men of the coast cheering while their enemy surrendered.

All eyes were on the Eagle-Bear, his beard glowing like fire in the light. All except Aiden.

Instead of Grímr and Einarr, he saw Hallvaror, face white as a sheet, pouring blood from his lethal gut wound, getting slowly to his feet, holding an axe— Aiden's axe— retrieved from the mud. Aiden shouted, and Hallvaror lunged as Arnnjorn turned. But Aiden, with impossible speed, got there first, raising his shield to stop that axe and, when it hooked on wood, he ripped the weapon from Hallvaror's broken fingers and smashed his shield into the side of the Jarl's head, driving him back to the ground with blow after blow. When at last he was still, Aiden stumbled backwards into Arnnjorn's chest. The chief caught him. He was saying something, maybe praise, maybe calling for help. Aiden couldn't hear anything but white noise. Everything hurt. That last image he'd seen of Grímr and Einarr burned in his mind. What if that was last time he'd ever see them alive?

"Aiden."

Einarr's voice cut through the fog, and Aiden looked up to see Grímr limping toward him, his arm around Einarr. Both of them were more hurt than Aiden had ever wanted to see them. But both of them were alive. If he'd had the energy, he would have cried. As it was, he just limped over to them and collapsed, knowing that, as long as he was in their arms, he would be safe.

Chapter Eighteen

It was several days before any of them were well enough to leave the tent where Yrsa and the other healers were still treating the injured, many of them from other towns, but not yet well enough to return home. But they refused to be separated. The three warriors stayed always within each other's sight. Aiden was afraid that, if he let them leave his side for even a moment, his nightmare would come true and he would never see them again. Gradually, like his injuries, the fear would fade.

After the last of Hallvaror's army was dealt with and the cleanup of the battle began, in the first calm moment, Arnnjorn came to them and praised all three of them for their heroics. And then, he let them know that there would still be judgement. Grímr had broken his outlawry by returning to town. Aiden and Einarr had committed treason by releasing a prisoner. He promised he would delay it until they were all well enough to bear the punishment, but it was not much reassurance to Aiden. After all this, would they only be separated again?

Eventually, they were moved to Yrsa's hall in Arnnstead, once most of the injured had been patched up enough to return home. Einarr was the worst injured of them. Hallvaror had nearly gutted him. He was going to have an impressive scar when it healed, but he'd live. Though Grímr had the most individual injuries of them, none of them were severe— the amount made them dangerous. Aiden was the only one facing permanent damage, however.

"I warned you about this leg," Yrsa tutted as she checked on it again. "It's not healing right. You'll probably have a limp the rest of your life, and you've only yourself to blame."

"I think Grímr is at least partially to blame," Einarr put in from where he was laying nearby.

"I'll make it up to him," Grímr declared, unbothered.

"How's that?"

"I'll carry him everywhere."

"For the rest of his life?"

"If he wants me to."

"What if I want to carry him?"

"We'll fight for it."

"Not in here, you won't," Yrsa said, smacking both of them with a wad of bandages. "If you're lively enough for that, make yourself useful and wash those."

The other two grumbled, but did as they were told, leaving Aiden to Yrsa, who was re-securing his leg.

"You're all doing much better," Yrsa observed. "Almost well enough to leave now."

The thought pleased Aiden for a moment, until he remembered what it meant. Yrsa finished with his leg and glanced out the open door to the well where Grímr and Einarr, bandaged and weak still, but recovering, were flicking water at each other instead of working. They'd been bed-ridden a while. The air was getting cool already, summer dwindling.

"It's going to be a short raiding season," Yrsa commented. "They've put it off so long while all this mess was sorted out. It'll be a miracle if they manage to sail out at all."

"Considering everything that happened," Aiden said thoughtfully, "It might be better not to tempt fate any more this year."

"Perhaps."

A quiet moment passed. The sound of insects humming and Einarr laughing drifted in from outside. The air was warm and sleepy.

"Those two," Yrsa asked, "Do you intend to stay with them?"

"What do you mean?" Aiden asked, confused.

"You're an odd bunch," she shrugged, unconcerned. "You and Einarr were hard enough for people to understand. But the three of you..."

"I know," Aiden sighed, reminded of this uncomfortable subject. He let the silence lie for a moment. It was dim inside the long, narrow medicine house. One of Yrsa's other patients shifted in his sleep. Grímr and Einarr would wear themselves out before long, their energy still sapped by recovering from their injuries, and would want a long afternoon nap in the warmth and the shade. Aiden reached for the wooden bead braided into his hair and gently pulled it off to look at it. Yrsa waited patiently for him to answer her question.

"For a little while," he said at last, turning the bead over in his hand, "I thought that, if I fought hard enough, worked harder than anyone, I could prove myself, and people would forget what I was. Where I came from. Who I love. But I don't think that's ever going to happen. No amount of great deeds will ever erase what they see when they look at me every day. So, I think, if they'll never accept me anyway, what's the point in not doing what I like? If nothing can change their minds, why not be happy?"

"That is a way to look at it." Yrsa pulled a pipe from her clothes and began filling it with the careless, memorized motions of habit. Soon, the spicy scent of her pipe weed filled the house, strange and sopophoric.

"So, yes," Aiden finished at last, fastening the bead into his hair again. "I'm going to stay with them. Both of them. No matter what."

"For what it's worth," Yrsa said, her eyes distant, watching the sea beyond her open doorway, "I hope you can. I truly do."

Einarr carried Aiden up to the washing spring one Saturday afternoon, and Grímr, as was his habit now, came after them without hesitation. Aiden's head was still full of Yrsa's words and worries about the future. He looked at Einarr and Grímr, who'd fallen easily into the routine of their old friendship, even now playful and easy as breathing. Grímr, stoic and often expressionless, seemed to melt only for two things— Einarr's easy humor and Aiden's tender, unselfconscious concern. There was no faster way to reduce the ragged outlaw to flustered frustration than to express genuine worry for him, or better yet, actually attempt to take care of him. He had no defenses for it.

Part of Aiden felt like Grímr had always belonged with them. He seemed to fill a gap Aiden had never noticed was there. When Aiden grew frustrated and snappish, Grímr could bring him out of it in a way that, if Einarr tried it, would only have irritated him more. And when Einarr grew close-mouthed and distant, hiding his obvious distress behind a smile, Grímr knew all the ways to open him up again. They fit each other. Aiden had expected it to end after that one desperate night when they were all worried they were on the verge of death. He had never expected it to feel this natural.

And that left him wondering what would happen once this was over. If Grímr was forced to return to his outlawry or worse. If they were separated... He found himself asking who he would follow. He loved Einarr, had loved him longer, wanted to spend his life with the man. But Grímr needed him. The outlaw couldn't be alone again. Aiden couldn't bear the thought of him sliding back into that feral place, living on in anger. But he had no idea what the other men felt. Would Grímr want to stay with them if the option was there?

"You're moping, little bird," Grímr spoke, interrupting Aiden's thoughts. "What has you so troubled?"

Aiden bit his lip, unsure how to word his fears. Einarr reached out across the warm water to move a curl of damp hair from Aiden's cheek and pull him closer.

"I'm not sure what this is," Aiden confessed at last, "The three of us. Is this... Can we stay like this?"

Einarr looked surprised, and glanced at Grímr for guidance. Grímr looked away, expression troubled by guilt.

"I don't want to come between you two." The water stirred as Grímr rubbed uncomfortably at his upper arm. "What happened, it could just be once. When we know what Arnnjorn's decided, I could just leave."

"Don't be ridiculous," Einarr said quickly. "You belong here with us. I mean, unless, leaving is what you want."

"I'm not sure what I want," Grímr admitted. "I don't suppose it means much to say I'm happier with you two than I've been in the last twenty years, considering what my last twenty years were like. But it's true. I don't want that to end, but..."

"Then don't let it end." Aiden took Grímr's hand, expression determined. "I've already made my decision. I want both of you. If that's possible, I won't let anything get in the way."

Einarr took a deep breath and nodded.

"Me as well," he said. "I want you with us as well. No matter what happens."

Grímr swallowed hard and looked away, still thinking. They let him be, going on with their bathing.

It wasn't until they were getting ready to get out of the spring that, as Aiden was climbing past Grímr onto the grass, the outlaw caught his hand.

"Wait," he said softly, "I want it. To be with you. Both of you."

Aiden smiled, and they stayed in the spring several hours longer than they'd meant to.

Chapter Nineteen

It wasn't long after that when all three men were called to the longhouse to stand before Arnnjorn and the other respected men of Arnnstead, who looked down on the three of them with solemn expressions. Aiden took a deep breath, telling himself Arnnjorn was sure to be merciful. Whatever happened, they would find a way to be together.

"You know the crimes of which you stand accused," Arnnjorn said, looking for the first time in Aiden's memory uncomfortable with his position as leader. "And you know the punishment they demand."

He turned his sober gaze on Grímr first.

"For an outlaw to return from banishment, he should be killed on sight."

Aiden tensed, holding his breath, ready to leap to Grímr's defense if necessary. Einarr put a hand on Aiden's shoulder to steady him.

"However, considering the length of your banishment, and the good you have done for us," Arnnjorn continued, "A dishonorable death would be a dire ingratitude. Instead, your punishment will be to resume your outlawry. As a show of thanks, you will be supplied and guaranteed safety until you are beyond our territory."

Aiden clenched his jaw, dismay tangling his insides. This wasn't right. Arnnjorn wasn't going to force them to split up. He had to understand that was impossible, right? He looked at Grímr pleadingly, hoping the other man would say something, but

Grímr's expression was resigned, staring into the distance with somber acceptance.

"Einarr, Aiden," Arnnjorn said next, "You committed treason against me. Disobeyed my direct orders and released a rightful prisoner. Once again, the punishment for disrespecting your chief in this way should be death."

Einarr's hand tightened on Aiden's shoulder, and Aiden knew Einarr would fight if that were the verdict brought down.

"But no crime should be judged outside of the context in which it was committed," Arnnjorn continued. "And your treason was in service of the greater good. Were it not for your choices, it is likely we would all be in the underworld now, rueing your obedience. I could not punish you for that. And yet, an example must be set. Such serious crimes cannot be seen to go without consequence. For that reason, outlawry is the only option."

Aiden's eyes widened in shock. He looked to Einarr, seeing the crushed look on his face. Einarr would have to leave his home, his family, everything he'd ever cared about behind. Aiden shook with guilt, realizing what this had cost the warrior.

"I sentence both of you," Arnnjorn declared at last, "To fjörbaugsgarður. To *partial* outlawry."

Aiden blinked, confused by the wording.

"Partial?" he repeated.

"For three years, you will be banished from all villages and settlements. No man may give you aid, and you will have no protection under the law. At the end of that time, you may return, your punishment served, and you will be welcomed back as brothers."

Aiden had not even known such a thing was possible. That Einarr would have to leave his family was still terrible, but at least it wasn't forever. And Grímr...

"In addition," Arnnjorn went on, "I would dispute the original sentencing of you, Grímr. Given your youth at the time, and the... ambiguity of the circumstances surrounding the death of which you are accused, I submit that complete outlawry was an unjust punishment. As chief, I reduce it partial outlawry. A further three years, and no more."

Aiden's eyes widened as he realized what Arnnjorn was doing for them. Gratitude overwhelmed him. He could feel Grímr shaking next to him, overcome by the first real hope he'd experienced in years. They would be able to stay together. There was a future for all of them.

That evening, Arnnjorn saw them to the edge of town.

"There's an abandoned farm," the chief said as he handed off a cart of supplies to Einarr, "in the valley beyond that mountain. It will need repairs. But it's better than starting from scratch. Be wary of every stranger. There are too many young men eager for the easy glory of slaying an outlaw."

Jódís was standing nearby, her face lined with grief, holding Agna in her arms. Agna hadn't stopped crying since she'd heard.

215

"It will only be three years," Einarr promised, trying to soothe her. "It's only like I'm going on a very long raid. In just three summers, I'll be back to see you again. So be strong and wait for me."

He was doing his best to act like nothing was wrong, but Aiden could hear the emotion in his voice as he struggled to hold back his tears.

"Don't worry," Grímr nodded to Arnnjorn, and to Jódís and Agna. "I know how to live in these hills alone. I'll look after both of them, and get them home safe to you in three years' time."

Faralder and Branulf had come out to say goodbye as well, and other friends of Einarr's. Faralder surprised Aiden with a hug.

"I'm going to miss you!" he cried. "Who will carve the mastheads for me now?"

"There are tons of men better at it than me," Aiden said with a small laugh. "You were always telling me I did it wrong."

"But none of them do it wrong in such interesting ways!" Faralder mourned until Branulf pushed him out of the way.

"Perhaps this is for the best," he said. "The three of you... the people aren't ready for it. But with time, maybe they will be. After all, if you could convince an old goat like me..."

Aiden smiled, and hugged the shorter man, though he protested.

They lingered a little longer, saying their goodbyes. As a final gift, Arnnjorn gave Grímr the horse which Grímr had 'borrowed' at Ingifast.

216

"She's more used to you now, anyway," Arnnjorn said with a laugh. "Doesn't listen to a damn thing I say. Take it in good health."

Grímr smiled, inclining his head in thanks. Einarr kissed Agna's head one last time, and together, the three men rode out into the hills, toward an uncertain future. Regardless of what happened, Aiden knew he'd be content. They were together. That was all that mattered.

48413585R00123

Made in the USA
San Bernardino, CA
25 April 2017